HOME ALONe 2™

LOST IN NEW YORK

Books by Todd Strasser

The Diving Bell

The Mall from Outer Space

The Complete Computer Popularity Program

Beyond the Reef

Friends Till the End

Home Alone Adaptation

LOST IN NEW YORK

A novelization by Todd Strasser
Based on the screenplay by John Hughes

SCHOLASTIC INC.
New York Toronto London Auckland Sydney

TWENTIETH CENTURY FOX PRESENTS A JOHN HUGHES PRODUCTION A CHRIS COLUMBUS FILM
MACAULAY CULKIN JOE PESCI DANIEL STERN HOME ALONE 2
FILM EDITOR RAJA GOSNELL PRODUCTION DESIGNER SANDY VENEZIANO DIRECTOR OF PHOTOGRAPHY JULIO MACAT EXECUTIVE PRODUCER MARK RADCLIFFE
WRITTEN AND PRODUCED BY JOHN HUGHES DIRECTED BY CHRIS COLUMBUS COLOR BY DELUXE®

These credits are tentative and subject to change.

12 11 10 9 8 7 6 5 4 3 2 1   2 3 4 5 6 7/9

Printed in the U.S.A.   40

First Scholastic printing, November 1992

For Adam, Matthew, and Maggie Brenner

PROLOGUE

On a cold, dark Illinois night, a police car stopped at a railroad crossing. The icicles hanging from the flashing crossing lights broke and fell as a long freight train rumbled past. In the back of the patrol car, Marv Murchens' head throbbed where old man Marley had smacked him with his snow shovel. Next to him, his partner Harry Lyme stared angrily ahead at the slow-moving boxcars. Harry's face was swollen and bruised, and the top of his head was raw where his hair had been burned away with a blowtorch.

All Marv could think about was that blond-haired McCallister kid grinning and waving as the cops put them into the back of the patrol car. If he ever got his hands on that kid again he'd . . . aw, what was the point? By the time they got out of prison the kid would probably be a grandfather.

Suddenly Harry nudged Marv and revealed a lock pick he had hidden in his hand. Marv grinned. Maybe they'd get that kid after all! While the cops sat in the front seat, listening to the loud clanking of the freight train, Harry picked the car door lock and the two bad guys quietly slipped away.

That night Kevin McCallister stayed up late cleaning his house. He picked up the toys the bad guys had slipped on, and went to get the electric barbecue starter, which was still hanging on the front door. He wished he could have seen Harry's face when he grabbed the red-hot doorknob.

Crash! Without warning, the door burst open and there stood Harry with a nasty, toothless grin on his face. Next to him, Marv was reaching for Kevin's throat.

"Merry Christmas, little fella!" Harry chuckled.

"Ho! Ho! Ho!" Marv imitated an evil Santa Claus.

Kevin didn't have time to ask how they escaped from the cops. He was still home alone and these guys wanted to carve him into little pieces. It was time to run!

"It's all over for you, pal!" Harry shouted as he and Marv raced after him.

"Yeah!" cried Marv. "You're all out of tricks, kid!"

Maybe not. Kevin dashed out the back of the house and ran through the snow to the side door of the garage. He managed to get inside just an instant before Marv reached the door. Kevin grabbed the remote garage door opener and then climbed up into the small storage attic that covered the back half of the ceiling above the cars.

Outside, Harry ran to the garage door. It was closed and the handle to open it was missing. As Harry stuck his finger in the hole where the handle used to be, Kevin pressed the automatic door opener. Suddenly the garage door began to rise. Harry tried to get his finger out, but it was stuck. The next thing he knew, he was rising along with the door!

Crash! Marv smashed the side window with his elbow, then reached inside and opened the door. Stepping into the garage, he looked up and saw two sneakered feet hanging over the edge of the storage attic. Thinking they were Kevin's, Marv grabbed them and pulled.

"I got him!" he shouted. But the body he pulled down wasn't Kevin's. It was a child-size mannequin. And there was a rope attached to it. Suddenly Marv heard an engine cough to life above him.

Behind Marv, trapped between the ceiling and the raised garage door, Harry watched the blades of an old self-propelled lawnmower begin to churn as the mower rolled toward the edge of the storage attic right over his partner's head.

"Marv!" Harry shouted. "Heads up!"

Marv looked up just in time to see the churning blades appear above. His eyes bulged and his mouth opened to let out a scream, but it was too late! The lawnmower tipped over the edge and came crashing down!

DECEMBER 1992
THE ILLINOIS STATE
PENITENTIARY
NIGHTTIME

"AHHHHHHHHHHH!" In a dark cell, Marv Murchens screamed in his sleep and woke up terrified. His heart was pounding and cold sweat poured down his face. He jumped out of bed and dashed across the cold concrete floor to his cell mate's bunk.

"Excuse me." Marv tapped the man on the shoulder.

"Whadya want?" snarled his cell mate, a huge brutish man, who thought Marv was a wimp.

"I just had a bad dream," Marv gasped. "Would you mind if I crawled in with you?"

Wham! The next thing Marv knew, he was sailing backwards. *Thunk!* Marv's head crashed into the wall and he sank down into his bunk, unconscious.

In a cell nearby, Harry Lyme heard his partner's head hit the wall with a sickening crack. Harry had also had a nightmare about the McCallister kid. The dream had ended with Harry looking up an old rain gutter and seeing a rusty ten-pound barbell come sailing down straight at his skull.

Harry slid out of his bunk and walked toward the thick bars at the front of his cell. His ulcer throbbed painfully in the pit of his stomach. He had a plan and, if it worked, both he and Marv would be busting out of this joint in a couple of days. Then they'd have to get some money and leave the country fast. Only one thing could slow them down. Harry's fists tightened around the cold steel bars of the cell. If he ever saw that McCallister kid again . . .

DECEMBER 22
OAK PARK, ILLINOIS
6 P.M.

The ground was covered with a white blanket of snow, and the houses were lit with colorful twinkling Christmas lights. On the outside, the large brick McCallister house resembled the other stately homes on the block, but inside was a tornado of pre-travel chaos as everyone rushed to pack for their holiday trip.

"Has anyone seen my sun block?" shouted Tracey, a pretty dark-haired high school senior, as she tried to get down the center stairs. Her path was blocked by her younger sister Sondra, who was lugging her snorkel and fins upstairs.

"What's the point of going to Florida if you're going to use sun block?" Sondra asked.

"Yeah," chimed Megan, who was trying to get

down the stairs behind Tracey. "I don't care if I age like an old suitcase, I'm getting toasted."

"So you'll just be a skag with a slightly darker shade of skin," said her older brother Buzz, who was big and wore his red hair in a flattop crewcut. Buzz was pushing his way up the stairs as if he thought he were Refrigerator Perry of the Chicago Bears.

"Buzz is jealous because he doesn't get tan," yelled Linnie, who was fourteen and blond. "His freckles just connect!"

At the base of the stairs, Fuller, the youngest member of the McCallister clan, watched the human logjam while sipping a can of Pepsi. Kevin had given him the soda after recording a big burp on his personal Talkboy tape recorder.

Now, a chubby, bald man with bad posture came into the room. His name was Frank and he was Fuller's father. That day he had driven his family from Ohio to Oak Park so that the McCallister clan could all travel together from O'Hare Airport the next morning.

"Hey," Frank said, waving a copy of the local newspaper at the crowd on the stairs. "Remember those robbers Kevin caught last Christmas? They just escaped from prison."

No one paid any attention, so Frank turned to Fuller. "Hey! Who gave you the Pepsi?"

"Kevin did," Fuller replied. "He said he didn't

8

care because we weren't sharing a bed tonight."

"You still better go easy on the fluids, pal, because the rubber sheets are already packed," Frank said. Then he looked at his watch. "Oops! Time to take a shower."

Fuller watched as his father started to push his way up the stairs. Jerk, he thought.

The only member of the McCallister clan who wasn't in a rush to prepare for the trip was Kevin. He was content to sit on the bed in his parents' bedroom and play with his Talkboy recorder while he watched TV.

Near him, Kate McCallister was busy packing. Kate was a pretty woman with reddish hair and too much on her mind. During a commercial for laundry detergent, Kevin turned to her.

"Mom," he said. "Do my ears stick out?"

"Of course not," Kate replied as she continued packing. "Whatever gave you that idea?"

"Buzz made fun of them," Kevin said.

"Well, I'll talk to him," Kate said.

Kevin sighed. His mother was always saying she'd talk to that big dork. Buzz always promised he'd change, but by the next day he'd be the same bully again.

"Aren't you nervous about your solo with the children's choir tonight?" Kate asked.

"That's the third time you've asked," Kevin

replied, annoyed that she was making such a big deal about the dumb Christmas pageant choir.

"I'm just concerned," his mother said.

"How come you're concerned if I'm not?" Kevin asked.

"I guess you're right." Kate shrugged and went into the bathroom to get her makeup kit. "Are you packed?" she called from inside the bathroom.

Kevin whispered something into his Talkboy and then quickly rewound it. "Yes, Mom," the Talkboy said.

"All the stuff I put out for you?" Kate asked from the bathroom.

Kevin played the Talkboy again. "Yes, Mom."

Kate came out of the bathroom with her brushes and makeup kit and laid them on the bed. "Oh, I forgot to show you what Grandma Penelope sent you for the trip."

Kevin rolled his eyes. She never got him anything good. "Donald Duck slippers?"

"Much better than that," Kate said, taking a plastic package out of her suitcase. "An inflatable clown for the pool."

"Just what I always wanted," Kevin groaned.

"Now, Kevin, you know it's not the present that's important," Kate said.

"Sure, Mom, it's the thought that counts." Kevin sighed. Did she really expect him to *be-*

lieve that old line? He turned back to the TV. Ben Brenner, the debonair host of Celebrity Ding-Dang-Dong! was waving good-bye to the television audience.

"And thanks for joining us," he said. "We'll see you tomorrow on the new Celebrity Ding-Dang-Dong!"

No, you won't, Kevin thought sadly, because I'll be in Florida in the sweltering heat and practically no ozone layer, playing with my new inflatable clown.

A grand-looking hotel came on the TV screen. It looked like a huge mansion with tall columns and flags in front. "Guests of the new Celebrity Ding-Dang-Dong! stay at the world renowned Plaza Hotel. It's New York's most exciting hotel experience. For reservations, call toll-free, 1-800-759-3000."

Now that would be a cool place to go, Kevin thought as his father, Peter, entered the bedroom carrying the family's silver Christmas bell ornament. Peter was a handsome man of medium height with short brown hair. Sometimes it was hard for Kevin to believe that he and Uncle Frank were actually brothers.

Ding! Ding! Peter shook the silver bell, and both Kate and Kevin looked up, recalling Christmas morning the year before.

"Every time I hear that bell I remember finding you home alone," Kate said with motherly

11

love in her eyes. "You were such a brave little boy."

"Sure, Mom." Kevin rolled his eyes. He was tired of hearing about what had happened last Christmas, when he captured those two dumb robbers. It wasn't right to dwell on the past. A kid had to get on with his life.

"I thought you'd like to take this along," Peter said, handing the bell to his wife.

"You're right." Kate packed it into her suitcase. Kevin turned back to the TV and started watching a news show about credit card fraud. A guy who looked like Karl Malden was saying that the illegal use of stolen credit cards was one of the fastest-growing areas of crime in the country and the police were really starting to crack down on the offenders of all ages. Suddenly Peter stepped right in front of the TV, blocking Kevin's view.

"Hey, look out!" Kevin said. "What're you doing, Dad?"

"Looking for the camcorder battery," Peter said.

"It's in the charger," Kate said.

Peter reached behind the nightstand and pulled out the multiple wall plug, not noticing that he was disconnecting the digital alarm clock on the night table. He removed the battery charger and replaced the plug in the wall socket. Instead of reading the correct time, the alarm

12

clock just flashed 12:00 over and over. Peter straightened up and turned to Kevin.

"Don't you think you better get your jacket and tie on?" he asked.

Kevin looked up from the TV. "No."

"We have to leave for the Christmas pageant in a few minutes," Peter said.

"My tie's in my room and I can't get it," Kevin said.

"Why not?" Kate asked.

"Because Uncle Frank's taking a shower in the kid's bathroom," Kevin explained.

Peter turned to his son. "Just run in and get your tie. It's okay."

Kevin turned off the TV. "Does Uncle Frank have a lot of muscles nobody knows about?"

"Only in his head, honey," Kate replied with a smile.

As Kevin left his parents' bedroom, he found his cousin Sondra and sister Megan dragging their suitcases down the hall.

"Where's your suitcase, Kevin?" Megan asked.

"In my room," Kevin said.

"Well, Dad said we have to have our suitcases down by the door before we go to the Christmas pageant," Megan the know-it-all said.

"Are you my new mother?" Kevin asked. He couldn't stand it when she nagged him.

13

"Remember what happened last year?" Sondra asked.

Kevin felt his teeth clench. He hated the way they all loved to remind him how he'd missed the trip to Paris and ruined the vacation for everyone. Instead of replying, Kevin aimed the Talkboy at the girls and pressed "play."

"Blurgh!" The loud belch he'd recorded earlier came out.

Megan wrinkled her nose. "You're totally nauseating!"

Kevin just laughed. The girls pulled their luggage past him and down the stairs. Kevin went to his room and pushed the door open. He could hear the shower running in the bathroom and Frank singing something about a "cool jerk."

Wow, I never knew anyone could sing so badly, Kevin thought. He snuck over to the bathroom door and pushed it open a little. Through the translucent curtain he could see Frank wiggling around as he sang. Kevin aimed the Talkboy toward his uncle and started to record the terrible off-key singing. Suddenly Frank noticed him and yanked the curtain aside.

"Get outta here, you nosy little jerk!" Frank shouted angrily. "Or I'll come out and slap you silly."

Kevin slammed the bathroom door, grabbed his tie, and raced out of the room. Didn't anyone have a sense of humor anymore?

DECEMBER 22
OAK PARK
ELEMENTARY SCHOOL
7 P.M.

A little while later Kevin stood with the children's choir on the stage at his school. Each member of the choir held a small glowing electric candle. Buzz stood on a riser behind Kevin, and behind Buzz was a row of Christmas trees. The auditorium was lit with holiday lights, and its walls were adorned with wreaths, ribbons, and ornaments. The seats were filled with families of the choir members, and Kevin spotted his parents sitting next to Uncle Frank and his wife, Aunt Leslie.

Down in front of the choir, Ms. Wickersham, the silver-haired music teacher who accompanied the choir on piano, smiled and nodded. The choir began to sing:

"Christmas tree, my Christmas tree
Lit up like a star
When I see my Christmas tree
Can loved ones be far?"

In the audience Kate watched Kevin and Buzz with great pleasure and pride. She was especially excited for Kevin.

"Kevin's solo is coming up," she whispered to Peter. "Tell Leslie."

Peter leaned to his sister-in-law, who was even chubbier than Frank and had frizzy bleached blonde hair. "Kevin's solo is coming up. Tell Frank."

Leslie leaned toward her husband, but saw that his head was tilted back, his eyes closed, and his mouth agape as he snored loudly.

"Wake up!" she hissed, smacking him on the arm.

"Wha — ?" Frank opened his eyes, startled.

"Kevin's going to do his solo," she whispered.

"Oh, great." Frank yawned and went back to sleep.

On the stage, the choir continued to sing:

"Christmas tree, I'm certain
Wherever I roam
The glow from your branches
Will light my way home."

Kevin swallowed nervously and straightened the knot of his tie. He'd never sung a solo before such a large crowd before. Behind him, Buzz was also aware that Kevin's big moment was approaching. As usual the little twerp was getting all the attention, and it ticked Buzz off. If only there was some way he could mess Kevin up . . .

Buzz had an idea, but it would take another electric candle. He grabbed one from the kid singing next to him, and smiled to himself. This was going to be good.

In front of the choir, Ms. Wickersham nodded at Kevin and winked. Kevin took a deep breath. This was it. His big solo. He began to sing:

> *"Christmas time means laughter*
> *Toboggans in the snow . . ."*

Some of the audience started to smile and giggle, but Kevin tried to ignore them and kept singing:

> *"Caroling together*
> *With faces all aglow . . ."*

No sooner were the words out of his mouth than a bunch of people burst out laughing. Kevin's ears burned with humiliation. Even Ms.

Wickersham was grinning. Kevin forced the next lines of the song out:

> *"Stockings on the mantle,*
> *A wreath on the door."*

By now most of the audience was howling with laughter. Even the other kids in the choir had joined in. Kevin couldn't believe how rude they were being. Could his singing really be that bad? And why did his ears feel so hot?

> *"And my merriest Christmas*
> *Needs just one thing more . . ."*

People were laughing and pointing at him. Suddenly Kevin began to suspect something and turned around. Buzz was holding two electric candles and grinning like an idiot. Now Kevin knew why his ears felt so hot. That big jerk had held the candles behind them, making Kevin's ears glow in the middle of his big solo!

Wham! Kevin slugged Buzz in the stomach. The big dummy lost his balance and fell into the other kids. The next thing Kevin knew, the whole choir started to collapse like a bunch of bowling pins. The Christmas trees and wreaths crashed down as kids grabbed for anything that would help them keep their balance. Finally the entire chorus fell in on itself, forming a writing mass of arms, legs, electric candles, and Christmas trees.

In the audience Kate McCallister closed her eyes and shook her head in despair. Why was it always her children who caused the worst scenes?

December 22
The McCallister Residence
8:30 p.m.

The entire clan was gathered in the living room. Buzz and Kevin sat in chairs in front of the fireplace, facing them. It was like being on trial, with Kate as the prosecutor and the rest of the family, the jury.

"Buzz, you're the oldest so you'll go first," Kate said.

Buzz stood up and cleared his throat. He stared down at the floor.

"I want to apologize to all of you for whatever displeasure I caused. And I want to apologize to my brother." Buzz turned to Kevin. "I'm sorry, Kevin. My prank was immature and ill-timed."

"Immature or not, it was pretty hilarious," Uncle Frank said. The other adults glared an-

20

grily at him and he sank down into his chair.

"I can assure you all that there will be absolutely no more shenanigans from me," Buzz continued with the most phony apology Kevin had ever heard. "Christmas is a sacred, happy, family, together, loving, caring, getting-along-time-of-year, and everybody in the family of man should go along with that. . . . Amen."

Kate smiled proudly. "That was very nice, Buzz."

Kevin's jaw dropped. He couldn't believe his mother had actually believed that garbage. Meanwhile, Buzz turned back to Kevin. When Buzz was certain no one else in the family could see him, he curled his lips back and grinned maliciously at Kevin, wiggling his retainer with his tongue.

"Try to beat that, you little trout sniffer," Buzz whispered. Then he sat down in his chair, looking repentant.

"Kevin?" Kate said. "What do *you* have to say?"

Kevin rose and stared at them. He couldn't believe that they'd bought all the lies Buzz had just told. Couldn't they see that Buzz was yanking their chains? As Kevin looked into their eager, expectant faces, he could see that they'd been totally conned.

Well, Kevin thought, I'm going to tell them the truth.

"I'm not sorry," he said defiantly. "I did what I did because Buzz humiliated me and, since he gets away with everything, I let him have it. And since you're all so stupid to believe his lies, I don't care if your idiotic Florida trip gets wrecked. Who wants to spend Christmas in a tropical climate anyway?"

A shocked silence fell over the McCallisters. Then Uncle Frank jumped up from his chair and pointed a threatening finger at Kevin. "You better not wreck my vacation, you little sourpuss. Your dad's paying good money for this trip."

Kevin just smirked. Typical, he thought, and then turned to leave.

"Stop, Kevin!" Kate shouted.

"If you walk out of here, you'll sleep in the attic!" his father yelled.

Kevin looked back at them and shrugged. "So what else is new?"

December 22
The Third Floor
9 p.m.

Kevin laid on the fold-out couch and stared up at the attic rafters. How could they ever believe Buzz? he thought angrily. What a bunch of jerks.

He heard footsteps on the stairs. That would be his mother, of course, coming up to yell at him.

A moment later Kate opened the door and entered the room. Kevin stared straight up at the rafters and ignored her.

"The last time we all tried to go on a trip, we had a problem that started just like this," Kate said.

"Yeah," Kevin said bitterly. "With me getting dumped on."

Kate crossed her arms firmly. "That isn't what happened last time and it isn't what's happening now. Your brother Buzz apologized to you."

"And when you couldn't see, he wiggled his retainer at me," Kevin said. "He didn't mean what he said. He was just kissing up to you."

"I'm sorry, Kevin, but I don't believe that," Kate replied. "You've been so negative lately. I wish you'd be more cooperative. Now, we're all getting on that airplane at ten o'clock tomorrow morning. Your father's spending a lot of money to take us to Florida."

"Great," Kevin snapped. "We're going to spend three and a half hours cooped up in an airplane just so we can see a bunch of palm trees and old people with bony legs."

It was obvious to Kate that her son wasn't ready to cooperate. "All right, Kevin. You sit up here for a while and think about it. When you're ready to apologize to Buzz and the rest of the family — "

"I'm not apologizing to Buzz," Kevin shouted. "I'd rather kiss a toilet seat."

"Then you can stay up here for the rest of the night."

"Fine," said Kevin. All the anger he was feeling spilled out. "I don't want to be down there anyway. I can't trust anybody in this family. And you know what? If I had my own money, I'd go on my own vacation. By myself. Alone.

Without any of you guys. And I'd have the most fun of my whole life."

"You got your wish last year," Kate warned him. "Maybe you'll get it again this year."

"I sure hope so!" Kevin yelled at her.

Kate gazed helplessly at her young son. She didn't understand what was troubling him. Maybe he just had to be left alone. She turned and went back down the stairs.

Kevin watched his mother leave. Then he looked up at the rafters. Someday I'm going to go away all by myself, he thought. No one will bother me, no one will make fun of me, no one will cause me any trouble.

DECEMBER 23
OAK PARK
9 A.M.

The morning sunlight peeked through the bedroom curtains. Kate lay under the covers, dreaming that she was lying on a large rubber raft in a clear blue pool. On a terrace beside her, Peter sat at an umbrella table, wearing a thick white robe, sipping freshly squeezed orange juice, and reading the paper. The children had gone to the beach for the day, and Kate was luxuriating in the peace and quiet.

Suddenly she heard a loud knocking sound.

"Hey! Anybody home?" a voice shouted. "Ya better hurry or you're gonna miss your plane!"

Plane? Kate thought as she started to wake.

Oh, no! Kate sat straight up in bed and stared at Peter in wide-eyed terror.

"We did it again!" They screamed simultaneously.

In a flash they burst out of bed and started to wake the others. Moments later the three-story house was a mass of hysteria as the McCallisters dressed and got ready to leave. Still pulling on a blouse and slacks, Kate ran to the bottom of the third-floor stairs.

"Kevin!" she shouted.

Kevin opened the door from the third floor and rubbed his sleepy eyes. "Yeah?"

"Get dressed!" Kate gasped. "We're not leaving you this time. And wear your warm blue coat. It's cold out."

"Sure, Mom." Kevin yawned.

A few minutes later the front door burst open and fourteen hastily dressed people dragged their luggage outside. Their shirttails flapped in the winter air, their shoelaces were untied and their coats unbuttoned as they hurried into the two airport vans waiting in the driveway.

Kate stood on the porch and directed traffic. "Our McCallisters in the first van, the other McCallisters in the second van!"

Uncle Frank came out of the house lugging a heavy suitcase. "I know I shouldn't complain about a free trip," he mumbled, "but you people give the worst wake-up calls!"

Kate grabbed him. "Do you have the plane tickets?"

"Leslie's in charge of the tickets," Uncle Frank said. "I'm in charge of hotel reservations."

Kate let him go. A second later Aunt Leslie rushed out of the house waving the airline tickets.

"Got 'em, Kate!" she gasped. Peter came next, panting for breath.

"Why is it that every time we go on a trip, we leave in a state of confusion?" he asked.

"We'll have all vacation to ponder that," Kate replied. "Do you think everyone's out?"

"I hope so."

"Okay," said Kate. "Lock up."

While her husband locked the front door, Kate ran to the van holding Frank and his family.

"Leslie!" she banged on the van's window.

"What?" Leslie rolled the window down.

"How many do you have?"

"Seven."

Kate ran to her van. She needed to count seven more heads. She started with herself and Peter, then added Buzz, Linnie, Megan, Jeff . . . Kate's jaw fell open. Only thirteen!

"Kevin!" she cried out in a panic.

Kevin stuck his head out from the front bucket seat and waved his boarding pass at her. "Cool your jets, Mom. And this time I'll carry my own ticket. Just in case you guys try and ditch me."

Kate breathed a huge sigh of relief.

"Everyone present and accounted for?" the van's driver asked.

"Yes," Kate said. "Go!"

The vans roared out of the driveway. Next stop, O'Hare Airport and their plane to Florida . . . if it hadn't left yet.

December 23
O'Hare Airport
9:55 a.m.

With five minutes left before departure time, both vans screeched to a stop in front of the American Airlines terminal. People and bags began pouring out of the vans' doors.

"Hurry everyone!" Peter shouted as skycaps in black and red uniforms quickly tagged the luggage and threw it onto baggage carts. The families rushed into the terminal, but Kevin lagged behind. The batteries in his Talkboy had run low.

"Dad." He tugged at his father's tan overcoat. "I need batteries."

"I don't have any," his father hastily replied, but Kevin knew that wasn't true. His father always carried extra batteries in his brown travel bag. Kevin reached for the bag.

"Not now," his father said, pulling it away.

"Come on." Kate tugged at the shoulder of Kevin's coat and guided him toward the doors. "Everyone to the plane. Let's go!"

"Wait a minute." Kevin pulled away. "I really need batteries."

Near him, the skycap handed Frank the stubs from the luggage tags. Then the man rubbed his thumb and fingers together.

"Oh, uh . . ." Frank patted his pockets. "Uh, Peter? Can you tip this guy? The smallest bill I have is a twenty. I'll pay you back of course."

Kevin had heard that one before. Peter put the brown travel bag on the baggage cart, took out his wallet, and gave the skycap his tip. Kevin waited until his father put his wallet back, then he quietly took the bag.

"What's our gate?" Peter asked, momentarily forgetting about the bag.

"E-fifteen. It's all the way at the end." The skycap looked at his watch. "You better run."

Peter ran inside and Kevin followed. The other McCallisters were jogging down the concourse ahead of them. Keeping one eye on his father's tan overcoat, Kevin unzipped the brown bag. Inside he found a Polaroid camera, his father's wallet, an address book, an envelope filled with cash, and a package of batteries.

I knew it, Kevin thought. Still following the tan overcoat, he tore open the package of batteries and started to replace the used ones in his Talkboy.

Kevin didn't realize that his father wasn't the only man in O'Hare Airport that morning wearing a tan overcoat. As Kevin concentrated on putting the new batteries in the Talkboy, another man in a tan overcoat stepped out of a snack bar and started to rush toward his plane. Kevin saw the tan overcoat and kept following.

As the man hurried through a gate and into a jetway, a blonde ticket agent took his boarding pass and added it to the others in her hand. As she started to close the jetway door, Kevin raced up.

"Wait for me!" he shouted. But as he hurried toward her, he tripped on his shoelace.

Oof! Kevin slammed into the ticket agent and a hundred and fifty boarding passes fell to the floor.

"Gosh, I'm sorry!" Kevin panted as he got up.

"Don't worry about it." The ticket agent kneeled down to pick up the passes. "Are you on this flight?"

"Yeah," Kevin said in a rush. "And so's my family. But they're already on the plane and I don't want to get left behind."

"Do you have your boarding pass?" the agent asked.

"It's . . ." Kevin pointed down at the boarding passes scattered all over the floor.

A man wearing green coveralls came up the jetway from the plane.

"We gotta close up here," he said. "They gotta go."

"But he dropped his boarding pass." The ticket agent pointed at Kevin.

"They can't leave!" Kevin cried. "This happened to me last year and it almost wrecked my Christmas."

"You're sure your family's on this flight?" the man asked.

Kevin nodded. "My dad got on just before I crashed into this lady."

"All right." The man turned to the ticket agent. "I guess you should board him and make sure he locates his family."

Kevin and the ticket agent hurried down the jetway and into the plane.

"Do you see your family?" the ticket agent asked.

The plane was a wide body and the aisles were crowded with people taking off their coats and putting carry-ons in the overhead bins. Kevin spotted the tan overcoat. The man wearing it had his back turned. "That's my dad."

"Good," said the ticket agent. "Take any open seat and have a Merry Christmas."

Kevin found a place to sit and put his blue coat in the overhead bin and his father's brown travel bag under the seat in front of him. He glanced around to see if any members of his family were sitting nearby, but the aisle was still crowded and he didn't see any familiar faces. That bothered him for a moment, but he decided they must've been spread around the plane in random seats. Kevin settled back and slipped on the earphones of his Talkboy. It was going to be a long, boring flight, and he figured he'd better entertain himself.

Not far away, another jet was also pulling away from its gate. In the first-class section Peter and Kate were still settling into their seats.

"I never thought we'd make it," Peter said as he sat back and relaxed. Next to him Kate bit her lip and furrowed her brow.

"Something wrong?" Peter asked.

"I don't know," Kate replied. "It's that feeling."

"That you forgot something?" Peter asked.

"I know I didn't," Kate said. "But I can't shake the feeling . . ."

Peter took her hand in his and squeezed. "It's just bad memories. That's all. We did everything, we brought everything. We're all here. There's nothing to worry about."

Kate smiled weakly and tried to relax. It had been a year since they'd all tried to take a Christmas vacation together. She just hoped this one would go better than the last.

DECEMBER 23
LaGuardia Airport
New York
11:30 a.m.

As his jet touched down on the runway, Kevin looked up in surprise. Wow, the time had really passed quickly. All around him people were getting up and filing out of the plane. Kevin got his coat and the brown travel bag, and walked up the jetway. He waited by the gate and looked for a familiar face. Dozens of people passed, but none of them were McCallisters. Finally the flight crew came out pulling their bags behind them. Kevin looked back into the jetway. It was empty.

That's weird, he thought. Where's my family? It was possible that they'd all been sitting in the front and had gotten off before him. But then why didn't they wait? Kevin started down the crowded concourse, searching every face he saw, but his family wasn't there. He ducked into the men's room and looked at the feet inside the stalls. One pair of shoes looked vaguely familiar.

"Dad?" he knocked on the stall.

"Get lost," a man's voice replied.

He knocked on another stall. "Uncle Frank?"

"Get outta here!"

Kevin left the men's room. He didn't understand it. They wouldn't just leave him. Not after what happened last year. Back on the concourse he noticed something else strange. Everyone was wearing coats and hats and gloves. Was Florida having a cold spell?

Kevin decided to go to the ticket counter. A ticket agent was speaking into a phone nestled on her shoulder while she typed on her computer. Standing on his tiptoes, Kevin could barely see her over the counter.

"Excuse me, ma'am." His words came out in a rush of nervousness. "How come it's so cold outside? Isn't it supposed to be in the seventies? And also, how come I don't see any palm trees or senior citizens in shorts?"

The ticket agent scowled at him. "I'll be with you in a minute." She turned back to her call.

Kevin sighed and lowered himself to the floor. He noticed that a wall of large picture windows lined the terminal. Through the windows he could see a city skyline looming in the distance.

Suddenly Kevin felt queasy. He turned back to the counter. The ticket agent was still on the phone, but he waved at her anyway. Finally she put her hand over the receiver.

"What is it now?" she asked irritably.

"I know you told me to wait, but this is an emergency." Kevin quickly pointed toward the picture windows. "What city is that back there?"

"New York," the agent said.

New York!!!?

Kevin's eyes went wide and he grabbed his head. "I did it again!"

The ticket agent stared over the counter at him. "Is something wrong?"

"Where's Florida?" Kevin quickly asked.

"About fifteen hundred miles that way." The agent pointed south.

Kevin was in a state of shock. He walked slowly toward the picture windows. There was no doubt that the city out there was New York. He could see the pointy top of the Empire State Building, and the World Trade Center towers looking like two long building blocks turned on end. It was unbelievable! His dumb family was in Florida. He was in New York.

Gradually, the shock began to wear off. That's right, he thought. Those jerks are in Florida . . . I'm in New York.

A big smile grew on Kevin's face. Hey! This could be great!

DECEMBER 23
MIAMI AIRPORT, FLORIDA
1:25 P.M.

The McCallister clan stood around the baggage carousel, staring out the windows. They could see a few palm trees and one or two senior citizens. But mostly they saw rain . . . thick sheets of it pouring down like a waterfall.

"Great way to start a vacation," Kate said with a sigh.

"Look at it this way," Peter said. "It can't get worse." The bags were starting to come down the chute and Kate turned back to the carousel.

"Everybody takes their own luggage!" she shouted.

As the first bag came around, Peter picked it up and read the name tag. "Give this to Kevin," he said, passing the bag to Kate, who gave it to Leslie.

"Give this to Kevin," Leslie said, giving the bag to Rod.

"This is for Kevin," said Rod, who gave the bag to Megan.

"It's Kevin's bag." Megan handed the bag to Fuller.

Fuller took the bag and turned to give it to Kevin, but Kevin wasn't there. Fuller turned to Brooke instead.

"Kevin's not here," he said, giving her the bag.

Brooke gave the bag to Sondra, who gave it to Linnie.

"Kevin's not here," Sondra said.

Linnie gave the bag to Kate, who was busy passing out the other bags.

"Kevin's not here," said Linnie.

"Kevin's not here," Kate said as she handed the bag back to Peter.

Peter stared at her. "What'd you say?"

"I said . . ." Kate's eyes went wide and she screamed. "Kevin!"

The Miami Airport police were housed in a small green cinder block office near the main terminal. Kate and Peter sat in two uncomfortable wooden chairs across a desk from a heavy-set, red-faced officer named Bennett, who was making notes on a yellow legal pad.

"Where did you last see your son?" Officer Bennett asked.

"In O'Hare Airport," Peter said. "We dropped the bags off curbside and he came into the terminal with us."

"Most people get separated at security checkpoints," Bennett said. "Are you sure he got through security?"

"I don't know," Kate said, looking quizzically at Peter.

"We were late for our plane," Peter explained. "Everyone ran to the gate."

Bennett nodded. "And when did you notice your son was missing, ma'am?"

"Uh, not until we picked up our baggage here," Kate said.

"I see." Bennett wrote something on the pad. "Has the boy ever run away from home?"

"Absolutely not," Peter said.

"Has he ever been in a situation where he's been on his own?" the police officer asked.

"As a matter of fact, this has happened before," Kate admitted with a nervous laugh. "It's sort of become a family tradition."

"Oddly enough we never lose our luggage," Peter added.

Bennett raised a curious eyebrow.

"He was left home by accident last year," Kate explained.

41

"That's what my wife meant about the family tradition," Peter added.

Officer Bennett nodded. "We'll call Chicago and notify them of the situation. The odds are that's where he is. It's very unlikely he'd be anywhere else."

DECEMBER 23
NEW YORK CITY
2 P.M.

In the backseat of a taxicab crawling through traffic, Kevin studied a New York City street map. He'd just visited the World Trade Center and done some sightseeing in Chinatown. Central Park was his next stop, but as he got out at the corner of 59th Street and Fifth Avenue, his attention was diverted by a grand-looking hotel with tall columns and polished brass doors. A well-dressed man in a gray topcoat and a woman wearing a fur were standing under the flag-lined portico.

"The Plaza Hotel." Kevin imitated Ben Brenner's voice. "New York's most exciting hotel experience!"

Kevin was just about to cross the street into

the park when he saw a woman with long stringy gray hair and dirty disheveled clothes coming toward him. A bunch of mangy New York pigeons were perched on her head and shoulders, and dozens more clustered on the sidewalk around her feet.

"Oh, sick!" Kevin was disgusted by the sight, and quickly turned away. He could visit Central Park later.

Not many blocks away two other recent arrivals to the Big Apple were taking in the sights. Wearing stolen clothes and wool caps, the escaped convicts Marv Murchens and Harry Lyme strolled through a bustling Manhattan fish market past dozens of white-coated workers unloading cargo from trucks.

Harry stopped and sniffed the cold winter air. "Smell that, Marv?"

Marv wrinkled his nose. "Yeah."

"You know what it is?" Harry asked.

"Fish." Marv replied, looking around.

"It's freedom," Harry said.

Marv scratched his head and sniffed again. "No, Harry, I'm telling you it's fish."

"It's freedom," Harry insisted. "And money."

Marv suspected the year they'd spent in jail had affected his partner's mind in strange ways, but he knew better than to argue.

"Okay. It's freedom and money. But it's also fish . . ." Marv pointed at a man pushing a hand truck loaded with crates of fresh cabbage. "And cabbage."

Harry gave Marv a look. Sometimes he couldn't believe how dumb the guy was. "Come on, let's get going."

"Where?" Marv asked.

"Someplace where it just smells of freedom, not fish," Harry said.

The two escaped convicts left the fish market and walked along a street lined with tall buildings.

"So what's the plan?" Marv asked as he wrapped some double-sided masking tape around his fingertips.

"We gotta get out of the country before the cops track us down," Harry said. "I figure we have time for one big score. Then we buy some phony passports and split for good."

Ahead of them on the sidewalk, a man wearing a fake white beard and a Santa suit was ringing a bell.

"Please contribute to the New York Children's Hospital," he said, pointing to a small bucket full of change on a folding table. As people passed they dropped coins into the bucket. As Marv and Harry passed, Marv stuck his hand into the bucket.

45

"How do you like that?" Marv asked a few steps later, showing Harry the coins stuck to the tape on his fingers.

Harry couldn't believe what he was seeing. Stuck to his partner's fingers was a dime and four pennies. "That's really smart, Marv. Bust out of jail, hop a truck, ride seven hundred miles to New York to swipe fourteen cents off a Santy Claus."

"Every little bit helps." Marv peeled the coins off. "And you know what? Now we got ourselves a new name. No more Wet Bandits. From now on, we're the Sticky Bandits."

"That's very cute," Harry said, rolling his eyes. It was moments like these that made him think he should be working alone.

Not far away, Kevin was also walking down the sidewalk, unable to get the memory of that disgusting pigeon lady out of his mind. It was so gross. Why would anyone let pigeons hang all over them like that? The thought made him shiver as he waited in a crowd of holiday shoppers for the light to change. The streets were backed up with traffic, and everyone was honking their horns. The "walk" light came on and Kevin followed the other pedestrians weaving in and out of the cars stuck in the intersection.

Across the street, Harry and Marv also stepped off the curb. Seconds later, in the middle of the intersection, Kevin squeezed between the

bumpers of two cars and brushed past the escaped cons. Suddenly Harry stopped and turned
around. He caught a glimpse of a kid with blond
hair.

Naw, he thought, it couldn't be.

"What's the matter?" Marv asked.

Harry shook his head. "Thought I saw something."

Marv looked over his shoulder. Seeing nothing, he turned and accidentally bumped into the
back of a woman wearing a short, dark coat.

The woman turned and glared at him. She had
straight blonde hair and sunglasses and looked
like a fashion model.

"Oh, uh, sorry," Marv automatically apologized. But when he saw how pretty she was, he
grinned.

Whap! She slapped him in the face and walked
away.

"Hey, Marv." Harry couldn't help smiling.
"Anyone ever tell you ya got less brains than a
toadstool?"

DECEMBER 23
MIAMI AIRPORT
2:30 P.M.

Officer Bennett was on the phone. On the other side of the desk, Kate tapped her fingers nervously and Peter gnawed on his thumbnail. Just because Kevin had miraculously defended himself against two vicious criminals at home the year before didn't mean he could survive on his own in O'Hare Airport.

Bennett hung up and shook his head. "Sorry, folks. The police at O'Hare haven't seen him."

Kate and Peter stared at each other. What if Kevin had been kidnapped? Kate slumped down in the chair, sick with worry. Peter placed a comforting hand on her shoulder.

"Do either of you have a recent photo of the boy?" Bennett asked.

"I have one." Peter reached into his pocket for his wallet, but it wasn't there. "My wallet's gone."

"Where could it be?" Kate asked.

"It was in my travel bag."

"Where's that?" Bennett asked.

Peter rubbed his chin and thought. "The last I remember, Kevin wanted it at the airport. He was looking for batteries."

"You think he took it?" Kate asked.

"I bet he did," Peter said.

"Then he could have your wallet," Bennett said. "Were there credit cards in it?"

"Sure," Peter said. "Credit cards, money, my address book, a camera . . ."

"We'll notify the credit card companies." Bennett picked up the phone and started dialing. "If your son uses any of the cards we'll be able to get a location on him."

Kate shook her head wearily. "I don't think Kevin even knows how to use a credit card."

December 23
The Plaza Hotel
3:00 P.M.

If Kevin was going to spend his vacation in New York, he'd need a place to stay. So why not try New York's most exciting hotel experience? As he stepped through the huge brass doors of the Plaza Hotel and into the lobby, he could see that this was his kind of place.

Several stories above him hung a giant crystal chandelier. The walls were covered with antique tapestries, and in tables all around him were elaborate floral displays in huge blue and white Chinese vases. Kevin pressed the "play" button on the Talkboy: *Guests of the new Celebrity Ding-Dang-Dong! stay at the world renowned*

Plaza Hotel. It's New York's most exciting hotel experience. For reservations call toll-free 1-800-759-3000."

Kevin clicked off the Talkboy and smiled. I'll do just that, he thought.

To the left of the lobby he found a row of telephones along one wall. Unfortunately, the phones were just out of reach. But Kevin quickly found a solution — he piled two thick phone books on the floor and stood on them. Getting the Plaza to accept a room reservation from a kid was going to take a bit of ingenuity, but with the help of his Talkboy, Kevin thought he could do it.

He had just finished preparing the Talkboy for the call when a woman wearing a gray suit and carrying a black leather briefcase stepped up to the phone next to his. Kevin noticed she was staring at him.

"You know, in bathrooms they have little toilets for kids," Kevin said. "I guess the people who make phone booths don't care as much about kids as the people who make toilets. Excuse me, I have a call to make."

The woman quickly moved several phones away. Kevin dialed the 800 number for room reservations and set the Talkboy next to the phone. As soon as the reservations agent answered, he hit the "play" button and pressed his finger against the cassette tape, slowing it down so that his voice sounded deep and mature.

"Hello, this is Peter McCallister. The father. I'd like to have a hotel room, please. With an extra large bed and a TV and one of those little refrigerators with food in it that you have to open with a key."

Kevin pressed the "pause" button.

"Do you have a credit card, sir?" the reservations agent asked.

Kevin pressed "play": *"A credit card? You got it."*

The next thing the reservations agent heard was the account number on Peter McCallister's Visa card. A few seconds later, Kevin had his reservation. Next stop: the hotel reception counter.

Kevin crossed the lobby. A workman with a buffing machine was polishing the floor and making it so slick Kevin slipped and almost fell.

"Watch it, son," the man said.

Kevin regained his balance and walked more carefully. On the other side of the lobby, the reception counter was even higher than the one at the airport. Kevin pulled himself up until he could see over it. A female clerk with reddish brown hair stared back at him curiously. From the gold plate on her black dress Kevin knew her name was Ms. Acivedo.

"Can I help you?" she asked.

"Reservation for McCallister," Kevin said.

"A reservation for yourself?" Ms. Acivedo frowned.

Kevin had anticipated that question. "Are you serious? My feet aren't even touching the ground. I'm not tall enough to look over this counter. Think about it. A kid coming into a hotel and making a reservation? Not on this planet, ma'am."

Ms. Acivedo's neatly plucked eyebrows rose. "I'm afraid I don't understand."

"I'm traveling with my dad," Kevin explained. "He's at a business meeting right now. I hate going to his meetings because he always makes me sit in the waiting room. So he dropped me off here and gave me his credit card. He said you should check me into the room so I don't get into mischief."

Kevin slid his father's Visa card across the counter and held his breath while Ms. Acivedo inspected it. She seemed to take a long time.

Oh-oh, he thought. Maybe I did something wrong. He was just getting ready to run when Ms. Acivedo slid the card into a small machine and imprinted a credit ticket. Then she handed the card back to him.

All right! Kevin slid the credit card into his pocket. It worked!

Ms. Acivedo called for a bellman. Then she turned again to Kevin. "Do you have any luggage?"

"Just these." Kevin held up the brown travel bag and his backpack.

Ms. Acivedo smiled. "I hope you'll enjoy your stay with us. And when your dad arrives remind him that he has to come down and sign a couple of things."

"My pleasure." Kevin smiled. "You've been most helpful."

A young bellman appeared at the counter. He was wearing a dark jacket with tails, a white shirt with a black bow tie, and white gloves.

"Please show young Mr. McCallister to his room," Ms. Acivedo said, handing the bellman a key.

"This way, sir." The bellman picked up the travel bag and backpack.

Cool, Kevin thought as he slid a stick of Juicy Fruit gum into his mouth and followed the bellman to an elevator. Seconds later they stepped out onto one of the upper floors. Kevin followed the bellman down the hall and into a large suite overlooking Central Park.

This is great! Kevin smiled as he walked across the living room and looked into the bedroom. Inside was a large TV, a minibar with a small refrigerator, and a bed that looked bigger than the one his parents had at home.

Kevin grinned. A huge bed, all for me!

He opened the refrigerated minibar. Inside was an assortment of drinks and snacks. Kevin smiled. How convenient!

Next he pushed open the bathroom door. Inside was a whirlpool bathtub, a shower, and a smaller TV. Luxurious! And spacious!

Kevin returned to the living room. The bellman was waiting by the door.

"Is the temperature all right for you, sir?" the bellman asked.

"It's okay," Kevin said.

"You know that there's a second door out to the hall from the bedroom in case you want to go out that way."

"Uh, thanks," Kevin replied. He sensed that the bellman was stalling, but he couldn't figure out why.

"You know how the TV works?" the bellman asked.

"I'm ten years old," Kevin said. "TV is my life."

"Of course." The bellman smiled. "Did you know that the hotel rents movies? Dial seventy-seven and they'll send up a catalog."

"Okay, great," Kevin said. But the bellman still didn't move from the door. Kevin didn't understand it.

"Well . . ." The bellman rubbed his thumb

against his fingers. Kevin remembered the sky-cap doing that at O'Hare Airport. Now he understood. The man wanted a tip. Kevin reached into his shirt, pulled out a stick of Juicy Fruit and gave it to him.

"And there's a lot more where that came from," he said with a wink.

"Uh, thank you, sir." The bellman smiled crookedly and left.

Since the Plaza was a luxury hotel, Kevin decided to investigate the amenities. After a rigorous cannonball session in the pool, he retired to the men's locker room to take some steam. Inside the steam room was a wooden three-tiered bench. Wrapped in a fluffy white towel, Kevin climbed up to the third tier and relaxed. Everything was going quite wonderfully until two men entered the steam room and took seats below him. The room was so cloudy that Kevin had only seen the tops of their heads. He doubted they'd even noticed him.

"I tell you," one of them said. "The marketing director over at Skilling and Ross is pretty great-looking."

"I know who you're talking about," said the other. "She's . . ."

"Excuse me," Kevin quickly interrupted. "If you guys are going to use bad words, I'll have to leave. I promised my grandmother I'd never listen to that kind of talk."

"Sorry," the first man said. "We didn't know you were in here."

"It's okay," Kevin replied.

"So, uh . . . you see the Christmas tree at Rockefeller Center this year?" the second man asked the first.

"Yeah," said the first. "It's bigger than ever."

They chatted for a few minutes more. Then the steam momentarily parted and Kevin caught a glimpse of something that puzzled him. "Uh, excuse me again."

The men turned around and looked up at him.

"Are you guys naked?" Kevin asked.

"Sure." The men smiled.

"I'm outta here!" Kevin was off the bench and out of the steam room in a flash.

December 23
Motel Two
Miami, Florida
9 P.M.

Rain pelted the windows. The motel room smelled like someone's basement. The walls were covered with peeling yellow wallpaper. There were black cigarette burns on the windowsill and in the faded orange carpet.

Sitting on the bed, Buzz stared out the window at the rusting car up on cinder blocks, the dead palm trees strung with fading Christmas lights, and the busted neon sign that had long since fallen down. Behind him Uncle Frank belched and scratched his stomach through his T-shirt.

"I swear, Buzz," he said. "This place sure didn't look this bad when your Aunt Leslie and I honeymooned here."

Buzz wished Uncle Frank would disappear.

Then, as if a miracle had occurred, Uncle Frank did leave. Buzz smiled to himself and continued to stare out through the rain. But a moment later the door opened again.

Darn it, Buzz thought. Why can't they leave me alone?

"Buzz?" It was his brother Jeff.

"What?" Buzz answered without turning around.

"You're really upset, huh?" Jeff sat down on the bed.

With his back to his brother, Buzz rolled his eyes. "Very."

"Are you crying?" Jeff asked gently like he was some kind of therapist or something.

Buzz smirked, but all Jeff saw were his brother's shoulders heave. "Not yet."

"It's not your fault Kevin's gone," Jeff said as he started to undress. "We were all lousy to him. But it's gonna be okay. He's a tough little guy. He'll make it . . . wherever he is."

Buzz nodded, but didn't reply. Jeff got into bed and turned off the light. "Try to get some sleep, Buzz. You'll go nuts staring out the window like that."

Buzz nodded again, but didn't take his eyes off the window. In a motel room across the way, there was a gorgeous woman. She'd neglected to pull her shade down. Now that Jeff had turned off the light, it was a lot easier to see her. Buzz smiled to himself. He'd have to thank his brother someday.

In the room next door, Kate also sat by a window. She had someone else in mind as she picked up the motel phone and dialed her home number.

As she listened to the phone ring on the other end, she stared at the dusty plastic Christmas tree the motel staff had put on the nicked coffee table. What a sad Christmas this was turning out to be.

Peter came out of the bathroom. He looked pale and his eyes were puffy. "Anything?"

Kate shook her head and hung up the phone. "I tried the house. I thought he might be home."

Peter slumped down on the bed next to her. "We'll just have to keep waiting."

"Do you think he's okay?" Kate's eyes were filled with hope and worry. Peter didn't want to disappoint her, so he nodded. But the truth was, neither of them knew.

December 23
The Plaza Hotel
10 p.m.

Kevin was stretched out on the king-size bed, eating a large hot fudge sundae and watching a black-and-white gangster tape he'd rented from the hotel.

Now this is a vacation! he thought with a big smile. On the TV screen a shapely woman let herself into a dimly lit room and tiptoed past the dark silhouette of a Christmas tree.

"Hold it right there!" a raspy voice ordered.

The startled woman gasped. "It's just me, Johnny."

The lights went on, revealing Johnny, a tough-looking man with greased back hair, wearing a satin smoking jacket. He was a gangster.

"I knew it was you, Carlotta," Johnny said. "I could smell ya gettin' off the elevator."

"It's gardenias, Johnny," Carlotta said nervously. "Your favorite."

Johnny didn't seem impressed. "You was here last night, too, wasn't ya?"

"No, I was singin' at the Blue Monkey last night," Carlotta replied.

On the bed, Kevin shook his head. "Don't listen to her, Johnny."

Johnny didn't. "No you wasn't. You was here."

"That's a dirty rotten lie, Johnny." Carlotta sounded hurt.

"Don't gimme that," Johnny snarled.

"No, no." Carlotta shook her head. "You got me all wrong."

"All right, I believe ya," Johnny said, reaching down behind his desk and bringing up a black machine gun. "But my tommy gun don't!"

"Johnny!" Carlotta gasped and trembled. "I'm all wool and a yard wide! You're the only duck in my pond!"

"Get down on your knees and tell me you love me." Johnny pointed the machine gun at the floor and Carlotta quickly dropped to one knee.

"Baby, I'm over the moon for you," Carlotta begged.

Johnny shook his head. "Ya gotta do better than that."

"If my love was an ocean, Lindy'd have to take

two airplanes to get across!" Carlotta cried.

Johnny was quiet for a moment. "Maybe I'm off my hinges, but I believe you," he said, raising his gun. "That's why I'm gonna let you go."

On the bed, Kevin stopped eating. "Forget it. She's rat bait."

On the screen, Johnny leveled the tommy gun at Carlotta. "You got to the count of three to get your lousy, lyin', low-down, four-flushin' carcass out that door. One! . . . Two! . . ."

Carlotta scrambled toward the door, but it was too late. The tommy gun roared and bright flashes of light burst from its muzzle. Kevin covered his eyes as Carlotta fell in a heap.

Johnny lowered the smoking tommy gun and grinned sadistically. "Merry Christmas, ya two-timin' floozy!"

Kevin turned off the TV and took a big breath. That was enough for now. Suddenly there was a sharp knock on the living room door. He'd been expecting trouble and it sounded like it had just arrived. Kevin quickly hopped off the bed, turned off the bedroom lights, and ran to the bathroom.

Now the doorbell was ringing. In the bathroom, Kevin turned on the shower full blast. He made sure the inflatable clown was in the right position behind the shower curtain, then took the strings he'd attached to the clown's arms and head and hid behind the sink with his Talkboy.

Back in the living room, the doorknob slowly turned and the door opened. A tall man in a dark suit peeked in. He was the hotel concierge. He was suspicious because the mysterious Mr. McCallister had never shown up to sign the credit card slip and hotel reservation papers. The concierge tiptoed through the dark living room and pushed the bedroom door. Kevin had left the bathroom door ajar. The concierge saw the light coming out and heard the sound of the running shower. He quietly stepped into the darkened bedroom.

Crouched behind the sink, Kevin pressed "play" on his Talkboy and Uncle Frank's off-key rendition of "Cool Jerk" began to fill the steamy room.

In the middle of the dark bedroom, the concierge froze and stared at the bathroom doorway. That wasn't a kid singing. He quietly crept toward the bathroom door and opened it just enough to look in.

Kevins started pulling on the strings that made the inflatable clown's arms and legs jerk, imitating the dance Uncle Frank had done. At the doorway, the concierge saw a shadow moving inside the steamed-up shower. He pushed the bathroom door open a little more. Suddenly Kevin had the clown spin around and shake one arm angrily.

"Get outta here, you nosy little jerk!" Frank's

voice shouted angrily out of the Talkboy. "Or I'll come out and slap you silly!"

The concierge's eyes went wide. The kid really did have a father! Knowing he could lose his job for sneaking into an occupied room, the concierge turned and hurried out of the bedroom.

Uhgg! He tripped over a wing chair in the living room and fell to his knees. A moment later he crawled out the door.

Kevin heard the concierge fall and the door shut. He came out from his hiding place and left the bathroom. In the bedroom he turned on the light and looked around to make sure nothing had been taken. The brown travel bag was lying on the bed and Kevin opened it just to make sure.

Everything was there. But instead of closing the bag, Kevin picked up his father's address book and thumbed through it. Under M he found:

McCallister, Rob
51 W. 95th Street
New York, NY

If Uncle Rob's back from Paris, he thought, I should pay him a visit. He usually gives pretty good presents.

Kevin dropped the address book back into the bag and took out his father's wallet. Inside was a family photo taken the previous spring. Buzz had him in a stranglehold, Jeff was making rabbit ears over his mother's head. His father was trying to look very formal with his arms on Megan's and Linnie's shoulders, but Megan was blowing a bubble and Linnie was yawning.

What a bunch of wahoo's, Kevin thought. Then he looked out the window at the vast, dark New York night. The streetlights in Central Park glowed and distant windows shimmered in the buildings that lined the park. Kevin imagined families being together inside those buildings. It was Christmas and his family was far away in Florida. They may have been wahoos, but they were his wahoos. For the first time since he'd gotten off the jet at La Guardia, Kevin felt an ache in his heart and knew he really missed them.

DECEMBER 24,
THE DAY BEFORE CHRISTMAS
THE PLAZA HOTEL
7:30 A.M.

Someone was knocking on his door.

"Okay, Mom, I'm coming," Kevin mumbled in his sleep. He opened his eyes and found himself in a strange room. The memory of the previous day rushed back at him. He wasn't home in Oak Park, he was alone in a hotel suite in New York.

Knock, knock.

"Uh, just a minute," Kevin yelled. He hopped out of bed and pulled on the fluffy white hotel bathrobe he'd worn to the pool the day before. It was sort of big and dragged behind him on the floor, but it would do.

Knock, knock, knock!

"Okay, coming." Kevin went to the door and opened it. Out in the hall, the bellman was holding a hanger with Kevin's undershorts cleaned and folded under plastic.

"Jeez! Don't flash these babies around. There could be girls on this floor." Kevin grabbed the hanger and pulled it inside the room. Then he stuck his head out and looked around. Fortunately the hall was empty.

"I was very careful, sir," the bellman assured him.

"When it comes to underwear, you can never be too careful," Kevin said. The bellman looked suitably humbled and Kevin felt a little sorry for him, so he gave him another stick of Juicy Fruit.

Back in the bathroom, Kevin took his time showering and then stood before the mirror and slowly combed his hair. Ahead loomed a long, empty day. Kevin was starting to realize that he wasn't crazy about vacationing alone, especially in a place where he'd never been and didn't know anyone. He would have called his parents, but he didn't know where in Miami they were staying, and even though he had a return ticket to Chicago, there was no sense in going home to an empty house on a block where all the neighbors were away for the holidays. So he'd just have to make the best of the situation.

At least staying at the Plaza had some rewards, like a bathroom counter covered with free stuff like combs and shavers and shampoos.

Kevin spied a blue bottle of after-shave lotion. It had been a year since he'd last tried this stuff, and he thought he was probably old enough for it now. He spilled some onto his hands and rubbed them against his face.

"*Yaaaahhhhh!*" His shrieks could be heard up and down the hall. Kevin quickly splashed cold water against his burning red cheeks and toweled them dry. Maybe he'd wait two years next time.

Free toiletries weren't the only complimentary services the hotel provided. A little while later, Kevin went down to the concierge's desk in the lobby. The concierge straightened his suit and greeted Kevin with a plastic smile.

"Is my transportation here?" Kevin asked.

"Out in front, sir," the concierge replied. "A limousine and a pizza. Compliments of the Plaza Hotel."

"New York's most exciting hotel experience." Kevin winked and started across the lobby.

"Uh, sir?" the concierge stopped him. "I do hope your father understands that last night I was simply checking the room to make sure everything was in order."

"He was pretty mad," Kevin replied. "He said he didn't come all the way to New York to get spied on."

The concierge swallowed. "Of course not. Will he be down soon?"

"He already left." Kevin lied smoothly.

"Oh." The concierge looked disappointed. "I would like to have offered my personal apology."

"If some guy looked at you in the shower, would you ever want to see him again?" Kevin asked.

"I suppose not," the concierge admitted.

"I don't think you'll see him for the rest of our trip," Kevin said. He turned away and hurried toward the front doors, hoping he had the concierge fooled. Behind him, the concierge watched and wondered. The kid's story sounded plausible, but something about it still bothered him. Stepping over to the reservations counter, he started to type some information on the computer. The first place he'd check was the credit card company. Maybe, just maybe, he could find an answer to this puzzle.

At the Wollman Skating Rink in Central Park, Marv and Harry sat on a wooden bench at the edge of the ice, enjoying their newfound freedom. Harry read the newspaper. Marv watched the skaters. Without warning, a pigeon settled on Harry's shoulder.

"Hey, get outa here!" Harry took a swipe at the bird with his paper and the pigeon flew away. "Jeez, you ever seen so many pigeons?"

Marv didn't answer. He was too busy concentrating on a young boy skating toward them.

Hanging from the boy's sleeves were a pair of blue mittens. As the boy came close, Marv reached out and grabbed one. The mittens were attached through the boy's jacket by a length of yarn, and as Marv pulled, the boy spun around like a top. A moment later the second mitten popped out. Marv waited while the boy stopped spinning and skated dizzily away. Then he turned to Harry.

"Mittens?" he asked, offering them to his partner.

"You wanna knock it off, Marv?" Harry was really annoyed with Marv's nickel-and-dime thefts.

"But they're wool," Marv said.

"Never mind the stupid mittens," Harry snapped. "We gotta face the facts. We don't got the tools to pull off a big robbery. Your banks, your jewelry stores . . ."

"Your art museums," Marv added.

"Exactly," Harry said. "They all take a good set of burglar's tools. Not only that, even if we had 'em and knocked off a big job, what would we do with the loot? We don't know no fences in New York."

"Looks pretty bad for us," Marv said, keeping his eye on a teenaged girl skating nearby. A long red scarf flapped in the breeze behind her.

"What we need is cash," said Harry.

As the girl skated past, Marv reached out and

gave the scarf a sharp yank. It was in his pocket before she crashed to the ice.

"How about hotels?" Marv asked as the girl lay on the ice, looking bewildered. "Tourists carry cash."

"With our luck we'd hold up some guy carrying traveler's checks," Harry said, thumbing through the paper. "I got a better idea. Look at all these Christmas ads. All these stores are open the day before Christmas, but they ain't gonna make deposits on Christmas Eve."

"So they gotta keep the cash in the store until the day after Christmas," Marv said.

"Right." Harry nodded. "Now what store is gonna do the most cash business on Christmas Eve that nobody's gonna think to rob?"

Marv scratched his head. "Liquor store?"

"No, dimwit, even nine-year-olds know how to rob liquor stores," Harry replied impatiently. "*This* is what I had in mind."

He pointed down at a large ad in the paper for Duncan's Toy Chest, the world-famous toy emporium.

"A toy store!" Marv gasped. "That's brilliant, Harry."

Harry grinned and his silver tooth glistened in the winter sun. "There's nobody dumb enough to knock off a toy store on Christmas Eve."

"There is now." Marv grinned back.

DECEMBER 24
NEW YORK CITY
9:30 A.M.

Kevin sat in the red leather seat of the long white stretch limo as it cruised slowly through the city. He had just finished his pizza breakfast, and was watching Pink Panther cartoons on the limo's TV. This is the life, he thought. Buzz, if only you could see me now.

As the limo turned up Fifth Avenue, Kevin glanced out the window and saw something that made his eyes bulge — an old building painted in bright blues, reds, and yellows with windows filled with amazing displays of Christmas toys. A sign above the door said:

DUNCAN'S TOY CHEST

Kevin quickly reached for the intercom that connected him to the driver. "Please drop me off here."

The limo pulled to the curb and the driver hopped out and opened Kevin's door. "When should I come back for you, sir?"

"What time is it now?" Kevin asked.

The driver checked his watch. "Nine-thirty, sir."

"How about three o'clock?" Kevin said.

"Three?" the driver frowned. "That's five and a half hours, sir."

"You're right," Kevin said. "Better make it three-thirty."

The driver looked puzzled, but he left. Kevin pulled his coat tight and walked through the cold air and into the toy store.

Inside he stopped and looked around. He'd never seen anything like it. The ground floor was two stories high and every inch was filled with toys. Model trains tooted and puffed white smoke as they raced along tracks mounted on the walls, and electric boats sailed around a giant, plastic water tank. A popcorn machine dispensed free popcorn, a soda fountain free soda. Best of all was the huge demonstration area where kids could sample all kinds of games and toys.

Wow, Kevin thought as he watched a radio-controlled model airplane circle over his head, coming to New York just could be the greatest accident of my life!

And without a moment's hesitation, he dove right in.

Kevin wasn't the only person from Illinois exploring Duncan's Toy Chest. On the second floor, where the tents, tree forts, and playground sets were on display, Marv and Harry stepped out of two large wooden playhouses.

"Nice house," Marv said, "just no bathroom."

"But perfect for us," Harry whispered as they strolled through the rest of the toy store. "Later on today we come back and hide inside these houses. Tonight when everybody leaves, we come out and empty the cash registers."

They passed a table displaying long, furry gorilla arms with soft pink fingers. Marv stopped and slid one over his hand like a long glove.

"Hey, Harry, check this out," he said, raising his new "gorilla" hand.

"Come on, dummy," Harry said, annoyed. "Quit messing around."

"But, Harry," Marv said. "This could be good for picking pockets. Watch, I'll pick my own pocket."

Marv reached around behind his back with the gorilla hand and tried to take his wallet out of his pocket. Unfortunately, his aim wasn't very good and he accidentally hit the woman standing behind him.

Marv heard a gasp and felt the gorilla glove get yanked off his hand. He spun around and came face to face with the pretty woman in the short, dark coat who'd smacked him in the street.

"Hey!" Marv grinned. "What a coincid —"

Ka-Pow! The woman pulled on the gorilla hand and smashed him in the face. The next thing Marv knew, he was lying on his back, gazing up at dozens of little gorilla hands floating above.

Harry kneeled down next to him. "Can I ask you a question?"

Marv slowly nodded.

"Did you have to go to school to learn to be this stupid?"

Downstairs, Kevin dropped an armful of toys onto the cashier's counter. Since no one was going to give him any Christmas presents, he decided he'd have to give them to himself. He'd picked out a pack of mini-robots, a bottle of Monster Sap Super Slippery Bath Bubbles, a jackknife, a Game Gear, and a stack of game cartridges.

A portly, red-cheeked old man with white hair stood behind the cash register. He was wearing a blue suit with a gold watch chain strung across the vest.

"Shopping alone?" he asked Kevin as he totaled up the purchase.

"In New York, sir?" Kevin replied without missing a beat. "Frankly, I'm afraid of my own shadow."

The man smiled. "I just wanted to make sure."

"That's very responsible of you," Kevin said.

"Thank you," the man said. "The total comes to twenty-three dollars and seventy-five cents."

Kevin opened the brown travel bag, found the envelope of cash, and pulled out two $20 bills.

"Oh, my," the man said, staring at the envelope. "Where did you get all that money?"

"I have a lot of grandmothers," Kevin said. He decided it might be best to change the subject. "You know, you have a really nice store here. One of the finest toy dealerships I've ever visited."

"Thank you," the man said with a smile.

Kevin wasn't sure why, but he felt comfortable talking to him, which wasn't always the case with grown-ups. "This Mr. Duncan must be a pretty nice guy to let kids come in his store and play with the toys. Most toy stores prohibit that."

"Well, he loves kids," the man said as he placed Kevin's toys in a bag. "Actually, he's going to donate all the money the store makes today to the Children's Hospital."

"Tonight?" Kevin asked. "Like on Christmas Eve?"

"It's not possible tonight," the man said. "He'll leave the money here in the store and take it to the hospital the day after Christmas."

"That's very generous of him," Kevin said.

"Children bring him a lot of joy," the man said. "As they do for anyone who appreciates them."

The thought of sick children in the Children's Hospital really tugged at Kevin's sense of Christmas spirit. He opened the envelope again and took out another $20 bill.

"I'm not supposed to spend this money," he said, giving it to the man, "but I have twenty dollars from shoveling snow and I can pay my mother back with that. So you can give this to Mr. Duncan. The hospital needs it more than me because I'll probably just spend it on stuff that rots my teeth and my mind."

"That's very sweet of you," the man said. He turned and pointed to a miniature Christmas tree adorned with small ceramic figurines from "The Twelve Days of Christmas." "In appreciation of your generosity, I'm going to let you select an object from that tree."

"For free?" Kevin was amazed.

"Absolutely," the man said with a smile. "And may I make a suggestion?"

"Sure."

78

"Take the two turtledoves."

"Both of them?" Kevin was doubly surprised.

The man nodded. "I'll tell you why. You should keep one and give the other to a person who's very special to you. Turtledoves are a symbol of friendship and love. So long as the two of you have your turtledoves, you'll be friends no matter how far away you might be. Even if you never see each other again, you'll still be friends."

"Wow." Kevin took both turtledoves from the tree. "I thought they were just part of a song."

"They are," the man said. "And for good reason."

"Gee, thanks." Kevin slipped the ornaments into his pocket and picked up his bag of toys.

"Merry Christmas," the man said.

"Merry Christmas to you, too." Kevin zipped up his coat. "And be sure and bundle up when you go outside. It's a little nippy."

The man waved and Kevin turned to go. As he got to the front door, he looked up and noticed a framed portrait on the wall. The white-haired man in the portrait looked exactly like the man he'd just spoken to. Under the portrait was a small gold plaque which said: *E. F. Duncan, founder.* Kevin looked back at the cash register, but the man was gone.

He looked back up at the portrait in wonder. Was the man he'd just spoken to E. F. Duncan?

DECEMBER 24
NEW YORK CITY
3:15 P.M.

As Harry and Marv pushed through the doors of Duncan's Toy Chest and out onto the sidewalk, Harry suddenly stopped and shaded his eyes from the bright mid-winter sun. "I don't believe what I'm seeing!"

"You've seen traffic before," Marv said. "They call it holiday congestion."

"No, you idiot. *Him!*" Harry pointed at Kevin, who was standing on the sidewalk in front of them, concentrating on his street map of the city.

"It can't be!" Marv gasped. "I must be seeing things!"

"No, you ain't," Harry said, a nasty smile growing on his lips. "I thought I saw him before.

80

Amazing ain't it? We escape from prison and come all the way to New York and who do we run into? The kid who put us in the can in the first place."

"But what's he doin' here?"

"Let's ask him," Harry said.

Now that he'd finished his Christmas shopping, Kevin was studying his map, trying to decide where the chauffeur should take him next. Suddenly he felt someone lurking beside him.

Kevin turned around and looked up into the faces of two grungy, but familiar-looking men. One was short and stocky with squinty eyes and a slightly hooked nose. His friend was taller and had a mustache and goatee. For a second Kevin couldn't place them. Then the shorter man smiled and his silver tooth glinted in the sunlight.

"Hiya, pal," Harry said.

Kevin felt his jaw drop. "You guys are supposed to be in jail."

"The warden gave us Christmas off for good behavior," Harry said.

"Too bad we're gonna disappoint him," Marv added, reaching for Kevin's neck.

"AAAHHHHHHHHHHH!" Kevin screamed and started to run. Harry and Marv chased after him, but the sidewalks were crowded with holiday shoppers. Being small, Kevin could cut through the pedestrians easier than the larger men who kept bumping into people and tripping over shopping bags.

Kevin dashed down the sidewalk as fast as his legs would carry him. Ahead he saw a street vendor selling fake pearl necklaces. Skidding to a stop, Kevin reached into the travel bag, grabbed some money, and quickly bought half a dozen necklaces.

Down the block Harry and Marv were bustling through the crowd, knocking people out of their way. As Kevin started to run again, he put each necklace in his mouth and bit down hard, breaking the string that held the fake pearls. Ahead was Fifty-ninth Street. Kevin raced across the pavement and scattered the loose pearls behind him.

A second later Harry and Marv started across the street and hit the pearls.

"Whoa!"

"Whoops!"

Both men lost their footing, flipped in the air, and crashed onto the street. Harry landed face first. Marv came down on his back. For a moment, neither man moved.

Kevin sprinted up to the Plaza Hotel. Under the portico, the concierge was waving good-bye to a couple while the bellman put their bags in a black limousine. Kevin ran up to the concierge.

"There's two guys chasing me," he gasped, pointing back down the street.

The concierge smiled maliciously and reached toward Kevin's pocket. "What's the problem? A store wouldn't take your stolen credit card?"

The next thing Kevin knew, the concierge took the card and grabbed Kevin by the collar. Suddenly Kevin remembered the guy on the TV show talking about the police cracking down on credit card fraud offenders of all ages. Oh no! he thought, they're gonna arrest me!

In a flash he twisted out of the concierge's grip and ran into the hotel.

"Stop that child!" Now the concierge and the bellman were chasing him. Ahead Kevin saw Ms. Acivedo step out from the reservations counter to block his path. Nearby, the hotel maintenance man was still buffing the floor. Just as Kevin reached Ms. Acivedo, he went into a baseball slide and slid under her legs. As he jumped up, he saw the concierge and bellman crash into her and fall into a heap. Kevin ran into the elevator and pressed the up button.

Out on Fifty-ninth Street, Marv and Harry rose stiffly from the asphalt.

"I can't believe we lost him," Marv groaned.

"We didn't," Harry said, pressing one hand into the small of his back and pointing with the other at the front of the Plaza. "He went into that hotel. And when he comes out — wham! We got him."

"What about his folks?" Marv asked as he rubbed his bruised elbows.

Harry grinned. "He ain't with his folks."

"How do you know?" Marv asked.

"How do I know?" Harry repeated irritably. "This is New York, nitwit. No parent in the world would let their kid walk around here alone."

DECEMBER 24
THE PLAZA HOTEL
4 P.M.

Kevin ran into his suite and locked the door behind him. He went into the bedroom and locked that door, too. He couldn't believe how many things had just gone wrong. The bad guys from Illinois had come out of nowhere and wanted to kill him *and* he'd been accused of credit card fraud. As far as he was concerned, this was the end of the vacation! It was time to go home! He opened his father's travel bag and took out the return plane ticket to Chicago. Then he took some bags of Doritos from the minibar and packed them into his backpack along with the Polaroid camera, his father's wallet, and the toys he'd bought at Duncan's Toy Chest. Finally he stuck the Talkboy in the pocket of his coat. Suddenly he heard the elevator doors open out in the hall. It was time to take evasive action!

Kevin turned on the television and the VCR, and grabbed the remote. The gangster movie started to play just as the door to the living room began to open. Kevin turned the TV's volume up high.

"Hold it right there!" the gangster on the tape shouted.

In the living room, the concierge, bellman, clerk, and two hotel security guards stopped, surprised by the tough adult voice.

"Uh, it's the concierge, sir," the concierge said nervously.

"I knew it was you — " the gangster's voice boomed. "I could smell ya gettin' off the elevator."

While the hotel employees stared wide-eyed at the door to the bedroom, Kevin pressed the "mute" button and skipped over Carlotta's reply on the tape.

"You was here last night, too, wasn't ya?" the gangster barked.

"Uh, yes, sir, I was," the concierge answered. Could this be a trick? He stepped closer to the bedroom door. It was open a few inches and he peeked in just enough to see a man's shadow on the wall. Recalling what happened the night before, the concierge quickly backed away.

He shook his head. "I'm terribly sorry. We're looking for a young man."

"All right," the gangster replied. "I believe ya, but . . . my tommy gun don't!"

At the words "tommy gun" the others looked at each other in horror.

"Get down on your knees and tell me you love me," the gangster demanded. In the bedroom Kevin hit the "pause" button on the remote and waited.

In the living room the hotel employees looked confused. Finally the concierge spoke. "Do you mean all of us, sir? Or just me?"

Kevin left the VCR on "pause." The concierge swallowed and turned to the others. "I think we better get on our knees."

They slowly sank to the floor. Then the concierge said, "I love you."

The bellman coughed. "Uh, me too."

Kevin hit "play" and the gangster barked angrily: "Ya gotta do better than that."

"We love you!" the terrified hotel employees gasped in unison.

Kevin grabbed the backpack and airline ticket and ran out the bedroom door to the hallway. From inside, he could hear the gangster on the tape say, "Maybe I'm off my hinges, but I believe you . . . That's why I'm gonna let you go. You got to the count of three to get your lousy, lyin', low-down, four-flushin' carcass out that door. One . . . two . . ."

Kevin heard a maniacal laugh and then the

rapid-fire sound of the machine gun. A split second later the hotel employees dove out the living room door and landed in a pile in the hallway. Down the corridor, Kevin quickly disappeared into a stairwell.

He ran down the stairs and then out into a service corridor lined with bags of dirty linens, a couple of broken chairs, and room service carts covered with dirty dishes. Ahead were two large swinging doors. As Kevin neared them, he felt the air grow colder and realized they must lead outside.

Kevin burst through the swinging doors, and into a large garage with a truck loading dock. He ran to the edge of the dock and jumped . . .

Right into the waiting arms of Harry and Marv.

"Nice of you to drop in, kid." Harry grinned as he twisted Kevin's arm behind his back.

A few minutes later Kevin found himself walking down Fifth Avenue in the middle of a crowd of last-minute shoppers. Harry and Marv each had a firm, but discreet grip on one of his arms.

"We spent a year in jail thinking we had the worst luck in the universe," Harry said in a low voice. "But we were wrong, little buddy."

"Yeah," Marv added. "Right now *you've* got the worst luck in the universe."

Kevin knew his future didn't look bright. These guys definitely planned to do something bad to him. He secretly reached into his coat pocket and pressed the "record" button on his Talkboy. Maybe someday someone would find it and learn what had happened to him.

"What are you guys doing in New York?" Kevin asked.

"We busted out of the joint, kid," Marv said proudly. "We ain't robbin' houses no more. We're robbin' toy stores. Tonight, we're hittin' Duncan's Toy Chest. Five floors of cash. Then we're gonna get us some phony passports and — "

"You wanna shut up, Marv?" Harry snapped.

"What's the difference?" Marv asked. "He ain't gonna tell nobody. Except maybe the fish."

"Let's just get him down to the subway tunnel," Harry said. "I'll feel a lot better when he's on ice."

Kevin reached into his pocket and felt his airline ticket. If he could get away from these guys, he'd go straight to the airport, get the first plane home, and never come back to New York again.

"Hey, what's this?" Marv suddenly grabbed Kevin's hand and pulled it out of his pocket.

"An airplane ticket?" Harry yanked the ticket out of Kevin's hand and read it. "One round trip to Miami, Florida. Hey, Marv, I think the squirt must've gotten on the wrong plane."

"So his family's probably in Florida," Marv said.

"Yeah!" Harry laughed and ripped the ticket into little pieces. "You won't be needing this no more, little dude. Know why? 'Cause American Airlines don't fly to the Promised Land!"

The bad guys laughed and their cloudy breaths filled the cold air. Kevin bit his lip and watched the torn pieces of ticket flutter to the sidewalk. Now what was he going to do? Suddenly he saw a policeman on a horse up ahead, but even as he tried to figure out a way to get the mounted cop's attention, he felt Harry and Marv squeeze his arms.

"I got a gun in my pocket," Harry whispered tensely. "You open your mouth to that cop and you'll be able to spit gum out through your forehead."

Kevin didn't have a chance as they walked past the policeman. Back in the crowds again, he felt the bad guys loosen their grip on his arms. This might be his last opportunity. An attractive-looking woman in a short, dark coat was walking in front of them. As they stopped at a light and the crowd pressed together on the corner, Kevin reached forward and pinched her.

At that moment, Marv's head was filled with delightful thoughts — like how he was going to get rid of the kid, and how he and Harry were gonna become instant millionaires after they

cleaned out Duncan's Toy Chest that night. The last thing on his mind was that pretty lady in the short, dark coat who'd decked him in the toy store that afternoon. So he was quite surprised when she suddenly spun around and faced him.

"You again?" Her eyes widened.

Marv smiled. He always knew he had an unusual affect on women. Then he noticed that she was making a fist and pulling it back. But this wasn't the affect he'd hoped for.

POW!

As Marv tumbled backward, he let go of Kevin's arm. Kevin quickly turned and socked Harry in the stomach with all his might.

"Uhhh!" The bad guy instantly grimaced and dropped to his knees. Kevin stared at his little fist in amazement. Then he grabbed his backpack and took off across the street.

The light changed and the pedestrians left the corner, leaving Marv on his back and Harry on his knees, his arms wrapped tightly around his stomach. Marv propped himself up on his elbows. "Where's the kid?"

"Headed for the park," Harry grimaced and pointed toward the trees.

"You okay?" Marv asked as he started to help Harry up.

"Would I be on my knees if I was okay?" Harry snapped. "He hit me in the ulcer."

Marv helped Harry to his feet and they ran

into the park, looking for Kevin. Ahead of them was a typical late afternoon Central Park scene: joggers, people walking dogs, a horse-drawn hansom cab waiting for a fare, and a group of schoolchildren wearing caps or hooded coats, going home after a field trip. Harry and Marv smiled. It was obvious where they would hide if they were a kid.

They waded through the crowd of children, yanking the hats and hoods off every boy who appeared to be Kevin's height. But none of them was Kevin.

"I don't get it," Marv said when they'd finished. "We checked every kid."

"We should have shot him when we had the chance," Harry grumbled, looking around at the trees and joggers. "I hate pulling a job knowing that kid's out on the loose."

"What can he do?" Marv asked. "Kids are helpless."

"Not that kid," Harry replied.

"Hey, he don't got a house full of dangerous goodies this time," Marv said. "He's alone, and he's in the park, and it's gonna be dark soon."

Harry saw that his partner was right. The sun was sinking behind the buildings to the west, leaving long shadows across the bare trees and bushes. Pretty soon it would be night.

"Grown men come in here and don't get out alive," Marv said.

"Yeah." Harry started to grin. He liked what he was hearing.

"Good luck, little fella!" he shouted, and then turned to Marv. "I think it's time we paid Duncan's Toy Chest another visit."

Curled up in the storage box behind the hansom cab, Kevin heard Harry's shout. It might've been a trick to get him to come out, so he stayed in his hiding place even longer. It was dark in the storage box and smelled like horses, but Kevin knew it was better than winding up in the bottom of the Hudson River.

A long time passed. Finally, when Kevin was certain the bad guys must've given up searching for him, he pushed up the lid of the storage box and peeked out. The sun had disappeared behind the buildings. The sky was gray and the park was dark and cold. All the joggers and dog walkers he'd seen before were gone. He climbed out of the box, stepped over a frozen puddle of water, and watched the mercury vapor streetlights in the park slowly start to glow. Kevin hugged himself and shivered. He was alone, without a place to stay that night, without a way to fly home or to Miami or anyplace else.

And it was Christmas Eve.

"I want to go home," he sniffed. "Mom, where are you?"

CHRISTMAS EVE
MIAMI, FLORIDA
4:35 P.M.

The rain poured down relentlessly. The motel room felt damp and smelled like wet towels left in the hamper too long. Kate sat on the bed staring at the dull black rotary phone on the chipped night table. In a chair nearby Peter was slumped down, snorting and twitching in a fitful sleep, while the kids sat around the flickering TV in the next room, watching *It's a Wonderful Life* in Spanish.

The phone rang and Kate grabbed it. "Yes?"

"It's Officer Bennett, ma'am. We've located your son."

"Ohmygosh!" Kate gasped and shook Peter's shoulder.

"What? What is it?" he asked groggily.

"It's Officer Bennett," Kate said. "They know where Kevin is."

"Where?" Peter sat up, instantly awake.

"Where?" Kate asked the police officer.

"New York City, ma'am," Officer Bennett replied. "He's wanted for unauthorized use of a credit card in the Plaza Hotel."

"What!?" Kate gasped.

"What!?" Peter gasped.

"He's wanted for unauthorized use of a credit card," Kate told her husband.

"I'm sure he only did it because he was scared," Kate told the police officer. "He's not a troublemaker."

"Who cares about that?" Peter asked. "Do they have him?"

"Do they have him?" Kate asked.

"I'm afraid not, ma'am," the officer said. "Some of the hotel people tried to question him about the card and he ran away."

The disappointed look on Kate's face said it all. "Darn it," Peter muttered.

"We'll catch the next flight," Kate told Officer Bennett. "And thank you so much for your help."

She hung up and looked sadly at her husband. "So we know he's in New York. By himself. I don't know whether to be thrilled or terrified."

"I wonder if he'd know enough to go to my brother's place?" Peter said.

"I thought they were in Paris?"

"They are. But maybe they have a house-sitter."

"Didn't you say they were in the middle of a major renovation?" Kate asked.

Peter nodded and sighed. "You're right. The place probably isn't even inhabitable right now."

Uncle Rob's house was on a dark side street about a block from Central Park. As Kevin walked along the cracked sidewalk, he could see that the neighborhood wasn't what he had expected. Instead of individual houses with lawns and trees like Oak Park, the houses here were actually three- and four-story brick buildings pressed right up next to each other. And there were no lawns at all. Just a small garden in front of each building. While some of the buildings had lights on inside and looked inhabited, others were nothing more than shadowy wrecks, with boarded-up windows and doorways blocked with cinder blocks.

Kevin stopped in front of Uncle Rob's house and felt his heart sink. The building was dark and boarded up. The whole first floor was hidden behind a scaffolding of loose wooden planks laid across a metal frame. A long yellow refuse chute ran down from the third floor to a big metal Dumpster on the street.

Kevin stared up at the brass knocker on the front door. On the slim chance that someone was actually inside, he climbed the concrete steps and knocked.

No one answered.

Kevin knocked again. When that didn't bring an answer, he pressed his nose against the first-floor window and looked inside. The place was a wreck. The walls had been stripped away, leaving a wooden framework. The floor had been ripped up, too, the bare beams covered here and there with large flat sheets of plywood. Scattered around the plywood were ladders, workmen's tools, coils of rope, bricks, and cans of paint and varnish.

Kevin backed away from the window and looked up and down the sidewalk. The street was dark and empty. Down at the corner some men carrying a loud radio shouted and laughed. Kevin shivered and felt a little scared. He kneeled down in front of the door and pushed open the mail slot.

"Hello? Uncle Rob? Anyone home?"

No one answered. It was hopeless. Kevin walked back down the front steps and started back down a street called Central Park West. He stayed on the west side of the street, where the buildings were, until he came to a corner and saw several men in tattered coats sifting through garbage bins for soda cans. Kevin glanced nervously across the street where a tall shadowy stone wall ran next to a dark sidewalk.

On the other side of the wall was Central Park. It looked scary on that side of the street, but there might be fewer people. So when the light changed, he crossed.

Kevin walked quickly down the sidewalk next to the wall. The wind made the branches of the trees rattle and throw gnarled shadows over him. Suddenly he tripped over something and looked down to find a dirty-looking man huddled in some ragged blankets.

"Hey, watch it!" the man shouted angrily.

Kevin jumped away and quickened his pace. His heart was pounding and his mouth felt dry.

Kevin started to run. He didn't want to be in this cold shadowy place with all these scary people. Suddenly he saw a cab parked at the curb.

"Hey, taxi!" he shouted. A second later he yanked open the door and jumped in. The cab was dark inside and Kevin could see only the silhouette of the driver's head and shoulders. He slid into the backseat and tried to catch his breath.

"Boy," he gasped," it's scary out there."

The cab's interior light went on and the cab driver slowly turned around. He had a pockmarked, unshaven face, a bent nose, cracked and bloodied lips, and eyes that were dull and cloudy. When he saw Kevin, he grinned, revealing pitted, discolored teeth.

"Ain't much better in here, bud," he said.

"*AAAhhhhhhh!*" Kevin screamed and jumped out of the cab. Desperate to get away from all those horrible people, he ran into the park and followed a trail through the trees that led to a large mass of dark gray rock rising out of the ground. Kevin found a deep gap between two boulders and squeezed in between them. The walls of rock around him were cold and uninviting, but he'd finally found a quiet place where he could catch his breath and be alone.

As he gasped for breath, he felt his stomach start to churn and growl. He realized he hadn't had anything to eat since the pizza in the limousine that morning. Opening his backpack, he took out a bag of Doritos and quickly tore it open.

Boy, he thought as he pressed a handful of corn chips into his mouth, I don't ever want to take a vacation like this again.

A "cooing" sound startled him and he turned to find a pigeon standing on the rock behind him. Kevin smiled. Well, at least this was one creature that didn't mean him any harm. Glad to have some company, he broke off a piece of a Dorito and held it out to the bird, who eyed it for a moment and then plucked it out of his hand.

"I guess you missed dinner, too," Kevin said. "My mother told me never to touch birds. Especially city birds. But you don't look so bad. At least you're nicer than the people around here."

The pigeon finished the Dorito and Kevin decided to give it another piece. But when he looked up, instead of one pigeon, there were now ten looking down at him from the top of the rock.

"Where'd you guys come from?" Kevin asked, surprised. The pigeons answered by cooing and Kevin knew what they wanted. He reached into his backpack, but there was only one bag of Doritos left.

"I hope I have enough for everybody," he said as he crumbled up the last of the corn chips. "How hungry are you guys?"

But instead of taking the crumbled chips, the pigeons started to fly away.

"Hey! Come back!" Kevin cried. "Where're you guys going?"

All the pigeons left except one.

"Well, at least you have some manners," Kevin said. He held out the Dorito crumbs, but instead of eating, the pigeon started to rise from the rock. Kevin couldn't understand how this was happening, especially since the bird wasn't flapping its wings. Then something began to appear under the pigeon's feet . . . knotted, filthy gray hair, a forehead streaked with grime, bushy eyebrows, then eyes!

"*Ahhhhhhhhh!*" Kevin screamed and jumped back. It was her! That crazy disgusting pigeon lady! He turned and tried to run, but his foot got caught in a crack between the rocks. Meanwhile the pigeon lady was coming closer. Kevin had never seen anything so disgusting. He tugged and tugged at his foot. Now she was reaching toward him with filthy, gnarled fingers. Kevin covered his face with his arms. What was she going to do?

CHRISTMAS EVE
CENTRAL PARK
5 P.M.

Kevin felt the pigeon lady's hand go around his ankle and push down gently until his foot was freed. Terrified, he took his hands away from his eyes to see what she was going to do next. But all she did was back away. Suddenly Kevin realized she hadn't meant him any harm. She'd only tried to help.

Curiosity replaced his fright. Kevin took a step toward her, but the pigeon lady looked nervous and backed away some more. Amazing, Kevin thought. She must be the only person in New York who's scared of me.

"I'm sorry I screamed in your face," he said. "You were just trying to help me, right?"

The pigeon lady nodded and took another step back. Kevin could see she was really nervous.

"I'm Kevin McCallister," he said. "Your birds are real nice."

The pigeon lady stopped backing away and stared curiously at him.

"I've seen you before," Kevin said. "You had pigeons all over you. At first it looked kind of scary, but if you think about it, it's not so bad. They must be all over you because they like you."

The pigeon lady blinked. Kevin wondered what she was thinking. Maybe she didn't like people talking to her. "Hey, if I'm bothering you, just tell me and I'll leave."

She started to open her mouth. Kevin thought she was going to say something, but at first no words came out. Then she said "no" in a voice so small Kevin could hardly hear it.

"You sure I'm not a pain?" Kevin asked.

The pigeon lady shook her head.

"Good." Kevin felt relieved. Then he became aware of other sounds around them, like a whole chorus of cooing birds. He looked up at the trees and saw the dark outlines of hundreds of pigeons on the bare branches.

"Will those pigeons come back on their own or do you have to call them?" he asked.

The pigeon lady looked up at the birds and

then reached into her pocket. She took out a handful of seeds and put them in Kevin's hand, motioning him to throw them.

"They hear it," she whispered.

Kevin threw the seed and it scattered over the rocks. Immediately, the pigeons swarmed down and started pecking.

"Hey, that's great!" Kevin said.

A crooked little smile appeared on the pigeon lady's face as they watched the birds feed. Then a chilly gust of wind blew past carrying old brown leaves and scraps of newspaper. Kevin shivered and wished he could get something warm to drink, but he didn't want to leave the only friend he had in New York City.

"It's pretty cold out," he said. "I could sure go for a hot cup of chocolate. How about you?"

The pigeon lady gave him a puzzled, uncertain look.

"Maybe you prefer coffee," Kevin said. "Either way it's my treat."

In a million years Kevin couldn't have imagined the place where the pigeon lady wanted to drink her coffee. After picking up cardboard take-out cups at a coffee shop, she led him up a fire escape alongside Radio City Music Hall. They climbed through a window near the roof and sat on a metal grating. As Kevin sipped his hot chocolate, he stared down through the grating at the stage below where a dozen ballerinas in fluffy white tutus twirled to music played by the orchestra.

"I've heard that music before, but I can't remember where," Kevin said, cradling the hot container in his hands.

"It's the *Nutcracker*," the pigeon lady said. "They do it every year around this time."

In their tutus, the ballerinas looked like swirling, spinning white flowers.

"It's nice," Kevin said.

"And warm," the pigeon lady added, cupping her coffee between her fingers.

Kevin looked back at the window they'd climbed in through. The panes were frosted with ice, and cold air was seeping in. "Is this where you live?" he asked.

"No," said the pigeon lady. "I have an apartment."

"Do you have any kids?"

The pigeon lady shook her head and looked down at her coffee. "I wanted them, but the man I loved fell out of love with me. It broke my heart. Every time a chance to be loved came by after that, I ran from it. You might say I stopped trusting people."

"No offense," Kevin said. "But that seems like a dumb thing to do."

"I was afraid of getting my heart broken again," the pigeon lady explained. "Sometimes you trust a person, and when things are down, they forget about you."

"Maybe they're just too busy," Kevin said. "Maybe they don't forget you, they just forget to remember you. I don't think people mean to forget."

The pigeon lady shrugged. "Maybe. But I'm just afraid if I trust anyone, I'll get hurt again."

"I can sort of understand that," Kevin said. "I used to have this really nice pair of roller skates and I was afraid that if I wore them, I'd wreck them. So I kept them in the box. And you know what happened?"

The pigeon lady shook her head.

"I outgrew them. I never got to use them out-side. Just a couple of times in my room."

"A person's feelings are a little different than skates," the pigeon lady said.

"But it's kind of the same thing," Kevin said. "If you aren't gonna use your heart . . . if you just keep it to yourself, maybe it'll be like my roller skates. By the time you do decide to use it, it may not be any good. So why not take a chance?"

The pigeon lady nodded. "There's some truth to that."

"I think so," said Kevin. "Your heart may still be broken, but it's not gone. If it was gone, you wouldn't be this nice."

106

The pigeon lady glanced back at the icy window and sighed. "It's been so long . . . I mean, it's been a couple of years since I even talked to someone."

"That's okay," Kevin said. "You're really good at it. You're not boring, you don't mumble or spit when you talk. You should do it more often. I think you'd just have to wear an outfit that didn't smell like pigeons."

The pigeon lady looked down at her dirty clothes as if seeing them for the first time. "I guess I was working pretty hard at keeping people away."

"I know what you mean," Kevin said. "I always think I'll have a lot of fun if I'm alone. But when there's no one around, it isn't fun at all. I don't care how much some people bug me, I'd rather be with somebody than by myself."

"So why are you alone on Christmas Eve?" the pigeon lady asked. "Did you get into trouble?"

Kevin nodded sheepishly.

"You did something wrong?"

"A lot of things," Kevin admitted

The pigeon lady studied him for a moment. "Did you know that a good deed erases a bad deed?"

"It's probably too late for that," Kevin said with a shrug. "I doubt I'd have time to do enough good deeds to erase all the bad things I did."

"You'll be fine," the pigeon lady said with a smile. "It's Christmas Eve. Good deeds count extra tonight."

Kevin's eyebrows rose. "They do?"

The pigeon lady nodded. "Why don't you think of the most important thing you can do for others right now and go do it."

Kevin wondered what that would be. It didn't seem like there was anything he could do here in New York, but maybe if he tried he could come up with something. He got up.

"I better go see what I can do," he said. "But listen, if I don't see you again, I hope everything comes out all right. And say good-bye to your birds for me, okay?"

"I will," the pigeon lady said.

"And if you need somebody to trust, it can be me," Kevin added. "I promise I won't forget to remember you."

"Don't make any promises you can't keep." The pigeon lady shook her finger at him. But then she winked.

"Merry Christmas." Kevin waved and started to climb out the window to the fire escape.

Back down on the dark sidewalk, Kevin tried to think of what he could do to help others. He saw an empty soda can lying on the curb and put it in a trash can, but that didn't seem like much of a good deed. He'd probably have to clean the whole city to erase all the bad stuff he'd done.

As he walked along, a big bright plastic Christmas star on the top of a nearby roof caught his eye. Curious, Kevin walked toward it until he found himself staring at a large brick building. A sign above the entrance said NEW YORK CHILDREN'S HOSPITAL.

Kevin stared up at the windows decorated with blinking Christmas lights. In one window a boy wearing a robe and pajamas rubbed a clear circle in the fogged pane and gazed outside. Kevin felt a pang in his heart. It was sad to think of kids his own age cooped up in a hospital on Christmas Eve, too sick to be home with their families. Of all the good deeds he could do, Kevin wished he could do something for the kids in that hospital.

Wait a minute . . . ! The bad guys were planning to rob Duncan's Toy Chest. Hadn't that gray-haired man said all the money in the store that night was going to this hospital? Kevin's eyes widened. The bad guys were going to steal the hospital's money!

Kevin clenched his fists in anger. It was bad to mess with sick kids, but to do it on Christmas was inexcusable! Now he knew what his good deed had to be. He had to stop those guys from robbing the toy store.

109

* * *

A little while later Kevin was walking back up Central Park West. He knew he didn't stand a chance battling the bad guys in the street. But in a house . . . *that* was a different story.

By the time he got to Uncle Rob's house Kevin had started to formulate a plan. It would be called OPERATION HO! HO! HO! and to make it work, he'd need the workmen's tools, glue, cans of paint and paint thinner, kerosene, bricks, rope . . . and Monster Sap Bath Bubbles.

CHRISTMAS EVE
THE PLAZA HOTEL
9:30 P.M.

Shortly after the plane from Miami landed at LaGuardia Airport in New York, a convoy of yellow cabs pulled up in front of the Plaza Hotel and the McCallisters jumped out.

"Hey, what about the fare, mister?" a cabbie shouted at Uncle Frank as he left his cab.

"Uh, how about a group discount?" Uncle Frank asked.

"Whatya talkin about?" The cabbie pointed angrily at his meter. "That's the fare, you gotta pay it."

Uncle Frank pretended to search his pockets. "Gee, I'm out of change. My brother Peter'll get it."

By the time Peter paid all the cab fares and got into the hotel, Kate was standing at the concierge's desk, red-faced and furious. On the other side stood the concierge and Ms. Acivedo, the clerk who'd checked Kevin into the hotel.

"What kind of hotel lets a child check in alone?" Kate demanded.

"The boy had a convincing story, a credit card, and a reservation," Ms. Acivedo stammered.

Kate glared at the clerk in disbelief and then turned to the concierge. "What kind of idiots do you have working for you?"

The concierge swallowed. "Uh, the finest in New York City, ma'am."

Kate felt her blood begin to boil. "It's Christmas Eve, and because of you my son is lost in one of the biggest cities in the world."

"I'm truly sorry, ma'am," the concierge apologized.

"You're going to be more than sorry," Peter said angrily. "After we find our son, I suggest you prepare yourself for a civil suit."

The concierge blanched. "Sir, you must understand that it was an innocent mistake. But in order to make it easier for you, we'd like to give you a complimentary suite here at the hotel for as long as it takes to find your son."

"Think you could make that two complimentary suites?" Uncle Frank asked.

"I suppose we could give you an extra large suite," the concierge said.

"Sounds fair," said Uncle Frank.

"Mom! Dad!" Jeff waved from the other end of the lobby. "The cops are here!"

Peter ran across the lobby, went out the main doors, and down the steps. Several police cars were parked outside. A moment later, Kate came out and stopped on the steps. As she stared at the lights of the city, she began to realize the enormity of the challenge that lay ahead. Somewhere out there, helpless, lost, and afraid, was her son.

It would have stunned Kate to learn that her son was only a few blocks away at that moment, his face pressed against the window of Duncan's Toy Chest. On the sidewalk next to him was a plank of wood, a can of paint, and a brick.

Inside, on the second floor, Marv and Harry let themselves out of their playhouses. The store was dimly lit and quiet. The two bad guys trotted down the unmoving escalator.

"Bars up!" Harry ordered cheerfully, pulling a crowbar from under his coat.

"Yes, sir!" Marv grinned and pulled out his crowbar.

On the first floor, they vaulted over the cashier's counter. Harry jammed his crowbar into a cash register and started to pry it open. *Sproing!* The cash drawer slid out, revealing thick wads of green currency.

"Look at all that moola!" Marv gasped.

"Must be Christmas." Harry winked happily.

Marv quickly ripped open the next register. It, too, was filled with cash. "There's more money in this place than I ever dreamed!"

"It makes you wonder why we spent so much time robbing houses!" Harry laughed with delight as he dumped the wads of bills into a green gym bag he'd taken from the sporting goods department.

"The amazing thing," said Marv, "is we're fugitives from the law, we're up to our elbows in cash money, and there ain't nobody who knows about it!"

Outside on the sidewalk, Kevin turned the paint can on its side and laid the plank of wood across it, creating a teeter-totter. Then he took an envelope out of his pocket. On it he'd written *To: Mr. Duncan (The Guy Who Owns This Store).* Inside was a special message. Using a rubber band, he wrapped the envelope around the brick.

Kevin looked through the window and watched as Harry and Marv gathered up all the money that was supposed to go to the kids at the Children's Hospital. This is it, he thought, taking a deep breath and watching a plume of vapor escape his lungs. There's no turning back. Another Christmas in the trenches.

He knocked on the window.

Inside, Harry and Marv looked up. As they

followed the sound with their eyes, they stared at the window in disbelief.

"He's back!" Marv gasped.

They watched in frozen horror as Kevin took the Polaroid camera out of his backpack and focused it. *Flash!* Before Harry and Marv had time to react, Kevin had taken a picture of them. Harry looked down. Both of his hands were filled with cash and he was standing in front of a broken cash register. Through the window they watched Kevin remove the photo and stick it in his backpack.

"He took our picture," Harry groaned.

"How's my hair look?" Marv asked.

"You idiot!" Harry shouted. "All he has to do is show the picture to the cops and we'll go away for life!"

"No way," Marv said confidently. "By the time the cops see that picture we'll be relaxing on a beach in some foreign country."

But Kevin wasn't finished. He picked up the brick.

"Oh, no!" Harry gasped. "I got a feeling the cops are gonna see that picture sooner than we thought!"

Kevin threw the brick. *CRASH!* The whole window shattered into tiny chunks of glass.

BRIIINNNGGGGG! A symphony of burglar alarms started ringing loudly. Kevin backed a safe distance away down the sidewalk.

"We gotta get outa here!" Harry shouted, grabbing the green gym bag filled with money. He vaulted over the window display and jumped through the open space where the window had been.

Bang! He landed on the wooden plank, slamming one end of it to the sidewalk. Harry looked down and saw the paint can under the plank. He smiled. The kid was up to his old tricks again.

"Nice try, kid!" Harry shouted. "Too bad I ain't that stupid!"

A second later Marv sailed through the window and landed on the high end of the plank, catapulting Harry into the air. Marv looked around for his partner. "Harry?"

Thunk! Harry hit the sidewalk on his back and lay there dazed.

Marv looked down at him and scowled. "Where were you?"

"Where do you think I was, numbskull!" Harry shouted. As Marv helped him off the sidewalk, there was another flash from Kevin's camera.

"He took another picture!" Marv yelled.

"We gotta get him!" Harry shouted.

Kevin started to run. In the distance, police sirens began to wail as they responded to the burglar alarms. Looking back, Kevin saw the bad guys chasing him. If he couldn't beat them to Uncle Rob's house, he was dead meat.

CHRISTMAS EVE
UNCLE ROB'S HOUSE
9:50 P.M.

As Kevin ran down the sidewalk toward his Uncle Rob's house, he could hear Harry and Marv huffing and puffing behind him. He quickly hopped into the Dumpster and crawled up the refuse chute to the third floor, then climbed one more set of stairs to the flat, asphalt roof. He ran to the edge of the building and looked down.

On the street below, Harry and Marv stopped and gasped for breath.

"Where is he?" Harry wheezed, looking around.

"I don't know," Marv replied, panting.

"I'm up here, you jerks!" Kevin waved down from the roof. "Come and get me!"

As the bad guys gawked up at him, Kevin

117

snapped another picture with the Polaroid. Harry turned to Marv and pulled out his crowbar.

"Bars up!" Harry ordered.

"Let's kill," Marv growled. He started toward the steps to the brownstone.

"Hold on, pea brain." Harry grabbed him by the collar. "Don't you remember we got busted last time because we underestimated that little bundle of misery? We don't go after him until we got a plan that's better than his plan."

"This ain't like last time, Harry," Marv replied. "This ain't his house. He's runnin' scared. He ain't got a plan."

Harry rolled his eyes. "May I do the thinking, please?"

He looked back up at Kevin. "Sonny? Nothing would thrill me more than to shoot you. Knocking off a youngster ain't gonna mean that much to me. You understand?"

On the roof, Kevin stared down without answering.

"But here's the deal," Harry continued. "Since I'm in a hurry, why don't you just throw down your camera, okay? We won't hurt you and you'll never see us again. Sound good?"

"Promise?" Kevin asked.

"Cross my heart," Harry said.

"Okay." Kevin put the camera down on the roof. Then he picked up a brick. Below, Harry stepped forward in anticipation. Behind him, Marv waited, picking his teeth with a toothpick.

"Give it to me, kid," Harry yelled.

Kevin launched the brick. *Clunk!* It smashed Marv on the head. Kevin smiled. *Direct hit!*

Marv was lying on the sidewalk. Little bricks were swirling in circles in front of his eyes and his head felt like it had swollen to twice its normal size. Harry bent over him and held up three fingers. "How many fingers am I holding up?"

Marv saw dozens of fingers floating in the air with the bricks. "Uh, twelve?"

Harry clenched his teeth and turned back to Kevin. That kid made him so mad. "Hey, kid!" he shouted. "You wanna throw bricks? Go ahead. Throw another one."

Kevin threw another brick. As it sailed down through the air, Harry dodged it. *Bonk!* Marv was just getting up from the street when the brick smashed him on the head and knocked him down again. Unaware that his partner had been hit, Harry stuck his tongue out at Kevin.

"If you can't do no better than that, kid, you're gonna lose!" Harry shouted. "Better try again."

Marv lay dazed on the street, watching more little bricks and fingers float around in the air. "Uh, Harry, no . . ." he groaned.

Too late . . . Kevin threw down another brick and again Harry jumped out of the way. *Sprong!* Marv got smashed in the head.

"You got any more?" Harry yelled up at Kevin.

Kevin held his fire. Harry turned and found Marv sprawled on the street. "Hey, come on, get up. How come you're still lying around?"

Harry's words sounded distant and faint. Marv opened his eyes and saw three of everything, including three more bricks sailing down at them. "Harry!" he gasped, pointing upward.

Harry turned and saw the brick coming. He ducked.

CLUNK! Marv got hit again. This one knocked him out.

Harry looked down at his unconscious partner. "Don't worry, Marv. That kid's dead. Nobody throws bricks at me and gets away with it."

Leaving Marv to recover from his headache, Harry snuck down an alley behind the brownstone. There he found another Dumpster filled with rubbish. Above it was a metal fire escape. If he snuck up the fire escape, Harry thought he might be able to take the kid by surprise. He climbed up on the Dumpster, but the bottom of the fire escape was just out of reach. Harry crouched down like a swimmer and then sprang forward. His hands went around the bottom wrung of the fire escape.

He would have held on, but Kevin had greased it.

Harry swung forward. The bottom wrung slipped out of his hands. Harry went down.

Thwamp! Harry hit the ground flat on his back.

Still dizzy from the bricks, Marv staggered up the front steps and tried to open the door, but the doorknob came off in his hand. There was a string attached to the knob. Marv pulled on it. Nothing happened. Marv frowned and pulled harder. Still nothing. Marv backed up against the door and gave the string a real hard yank.

The string was connected to a staple gun aimed through the key hole.

Zing! Zing! Zing!

"YEEEEEEAAAHH!!!" Marv screamed and grabbed his rear end. He had just stapled his pants to his behind. As he spun around, the string went tight again.

Zing! Zing! Zing! Marv caught three more staples in the hip and doubled over in agony.

Zing! Zing! Zing! The last three staples stapled Marv's hat to his head.

In the back, Harry slowly rose to his feet and stepped onto the back porch. He tried the rear door, but the door knob spun loosely in his hand.

The kid must have disconnected it.

"You're gonna have to do better than that!" Harry shouted and gave the door a ferocious kick.

Little did he know that Kevin had tied a cord from the top of the door to the zipper of a plumber's bag hanging upside down over the porch.

Ziiiiippppp! When the door flew back, it pulled the zipper open.

Bonk! Clank! Plunk! A dozen heavy iron plumbers wrenches crashed down on Harry's head.

Marv grabbed his hat with both hands and pulled, but it wouldn't leave his head. He pulled harder. *Riipppp!* The hat came off, along with several pieces of pink scalp. Marv's face turned red with pain and anger.

"That's it!" he shouted. "I'm coming in!"

Marv hit the front door with his shoulder. The door burst open and he flew into the house. Kevin had pulled away the sheets of plywood covering the floor joists. Marv fell straight through the beams and into the basement.

CRUNCH! He hit the floor and laid there for a moment. Okay, at least he was in the basement and couldn't fall any further. A bit unsteadily, he rose to his feet.

And promptly fell again.

What the . . . ? Marv tried to get up again. His feet started to slide out from under him and he had to grab an old chair for support. He gave the floor a closer look. It was glistening. The kid must've spread some kind of liquid soap on the ground. Smart, but not smart enough. Marv spotted a large steel cabinet a few feet away. Its shelves were filled with paint cans. All he had to do was get to it, and then he'd be able to hold on and make his way across the floor.

Slipping and skidding, Marv managed to grab the edge of the cabinet. Suddenly it started to tip.

KER-SPLASH! A dozen open paint cans crashed down, knocking him to the floor. A few moments later, Marv staggered to his feet, drenched with thick gooey paint. It had soaked through his clothes, plastered down his hair, and was stinging his eyes. Groping blindly for something to wipe his eyes with, he felt a piece of cheesecloth and pressed it against his face.

Marv started to pull the cloth away, but it wouldn't come off. "What the . . . ?" The kid must've put glue on the cloth! Marv gripped it firmly with both hands and yanked in frustration.

Riiippppp! The cloth pulled free.

"*Yeow!*" Marv felt like he'd ripped half his face off. He looked down at the cloth and gasped.

Staring back at him from the cloth were his eyebrows, mustache, and goatee.

On the back porch, Harry crawled out from under the pile of wrenches. His head throbbed and he was nearly blind with rage. He limped into the dark house, feeling his way through a butler's pantry until he came across a light string hanging from the ceiling. Remembering how the kid liked to booby-trap things, he tugged the string and then quickly jumped back.

A bare light bulb flashed on. Harry waited to see what else would happen. No wrenches fell out of the ceiling. No fans blowing feathers started blowing. Harry smiled. He entered a hallway and found another light string. He pulled it and another bulb flashed on. Harry waited to see what surprise the kid had hooked up to this one, but again nothing happened.

So far, so good. Harry stepped into a small bathroom. There was a strong smell of paint thinner in the air. He saw another light string and pulled it.

Fiiisshhhttt! Another light went on. Harry felt his head growing hot. He looked up at the ceiling. Instead of a bare light bulb, he found himself staring at the blue-orange flame of a butane torch. Now he knew why his head felt hot . . . because his hat was on fire!

Harry couldn't believe it. The same thing had

happened to him last year! He quickly twisted the hot and cold water knobs on the sink, but no water came out of the faucet. Meanwhile his head was burning up! He had to find water! Looking around desperately, he saw the light reflecting off the fluid in the toilet bowl. Stick his head in the toilet? What choice did he have? Harry quickly did a headstand and dunked his flaming head.

FA-WHAPPPP! The toilet bowl erupted in flames. The flash of light was so great it lit up the entire brownstone. Harry straightened up and stared at himself in the mirror. Smoke rose from his head and his hat had been reduced to a few blackened embers. His face was covered with dark soot and the collar of his coat was smoldering. Now he knew why the bathroom had smelled of paint thinner. Because the kid had filled the toilet bowl with it.

Drenched to the bone, and standing in a huge puddle of paint, Marv looked for a way out of the basement. His eyes fixed on a rope hanging down through the bare beams from the first floor. Marv knew he could pull himself out of the basement with it, but only if it wasn't another trap set by that lousy kid.

He reached for the rope, gave it a little tug and then quickly stepped back. Nothing happened. He stepped forward and tugged it harder.

Again nothing happened. Filled with hope, Marv grabbed the rope with both hands, took a deep breath, and started to pull himself up.

Suddenly, something gave above him. The rope came loose and started spooling down. Marv looked up just in time to see a seventy-five-pound bag of plaster hurtling down through the beams.

Ker-Pow! The bag hit Marv on the head and burst into a cloud of white dust as it drove him to the basement floor.

A few moments later Marv pushed himself up. The white powder had stuck to the wet paint, making him look like a snowman on its knees. He spit out a mouthful of plaster and made two angry fists. He was going to murder that kid!

CHRISTMAS EVE
UNCLE ROB'S HOUSE
10:15 P.M.

On the first floor, Kevin stood near the double wooden doors that led to the living room. He had heard the explosion when Harry dunked his burning head in the toilet filled with paint thinner. He'd listened to the crash when Marv pulled the bag of plaster down on himself. Things were going just as planned, but now it was time to draw the bad guys upstairs. He cupped his hands over his mouth and shouted, "Don't you guys know that a kid always wins against two idiots?"

In the bathroom where he was trying to rub the black spot off his teeth, Harry heard Kevin and quickly dashed out. In the basement, Marv threw the rope over the beams and started to pull himself up through the floor. Above, he caught a glimpse of Kevin's sneakers.

"Harry!" he shouted. "The kid's in the living room!"

Kevin quickly scrambled up a ladder leading through a hole in the living room ceiling. But not before Harry burst through the double doors and saw him. Harry ran to the ladder and started to follow Kevin up. He didn't know that Kevin had sawed the ladder halfway through just where it pressed against the ceiling. It was still strong enough to support a kid's weight, but not an adult's.

Snap! Just as Harry reached the ceiling, the ladder broke in two. For a second Harry and the lower end of the ladder balanced motionless in the air. Then *Whomp!* Harry and the ladder slammed to the living room floor.

Marv ran in and found his partner lying on the floor with the ladder under him. "What happened?"

"What do you think happened?" Harry yelled angrily. "He cut the ladder."

Meanwhile Kevin leaned over the hole in the ceiling and waved down. "Hey, guys, why don't you try the stairs?"

Harry and Marv ran out of the room. Marv was just about to run up the stairs when Harry grabbed his arm.

"Hold on," he whispered. "Don't you remember what happened last time?"

Marv thought for a second. "Oh, yeah. The paint cans tied to the ropes."

"Right. Now watch." Harry jumped on the first step and stamped his feet as if he were going up. Then he jumped back down. A second later, a paint can tied to a rope swung down the staircase.

"OW!" Harry shouted, pretending it had hit him. Then he turned and winked at Marv. "That's one," he whispered.

Marv chuckled, then jumped on the stairs and stamped his feet, shouting, "Don't worry, Harry, I'll get him!"

He jumped off the steps just before the second can swung down.

"OW!" Marv shouted, pretending he'd also been hit. Then he whispered to Harry, "That's two!"

"Now he thinks we've both been clocked," Harry whispered back. "Let's go."

They started to run up the stairs. At the top, Kevin waited, holding a four-foot-length of iron sewage pipe over his head. Harry and Marv saw him and froze on the steps. Kevin swung the pipe down.

"*Ahhhhhhh!*" the bad guys shouted in unison.

PWHAM! The pipe hit them.

Thunk-a-thunk-a-thunk! They both tumbled backwards down the stairs to the first floor.

Crash! They fell through the open beams and into the basement.

Marv opened his eyes. He was lying on his back on the basement floor again. Dozens of little sewer pipes floated in the air above him.

"That's three," he groaned.

At the top of the stairs, Kevin cut the rope tied to the sewage pipe.

Clang! Clang! Clang! The pipe banged down the stairs and teetered momentarily on the edge of the beam over the basement.

Harry and Marv slowly got to their feet. Suddenly Harry looked up, saw the pipe, and gasped. "Don't move!"

A split second later the pipe rolled off the beam.

BONK! Both bad guys crashed to the basement floor again . . . with the pipe resting on their chests.

"That's four," Marv said groggily as he lay on his back again.

"Maybe we should've moved," Harry moaned.

The staircase from the second to third floors had doors on either end. The doorknob was missing on the second-floor door and Kevin threaded some rope through the hole where it had been, and made a loop. He could hear the bad guys starting to climb out of the basement again.

"Don't you guys give up?" Kevin taunted them.

"No way!" Marv shouted as he and Harry charged up the first-floor stairs, shielding their heads with their arms in case Kevin sent down another sewage pipe.

"You better say every prayer you ever heard, kid!" Harry yelled.

"Yeah!" Marv added. "I hope your parents got you a tombstone for Christmas!"

Kevin ran up to the third floor and rolled a big metal tool chest to the edge of the stairs. The tool chest was the size of a dishwasher, and he tied it to the rope that went down the stairs and through the hole in the second-floor door.

"I'm up here and I'm really scared!" He shouted with a laugh.

Harry and Marv stopped at the door at the bottom of the stairs. Harry grabbed for the doorknob, but got the rope loop instead. Too angry to think, he gave the rope a mighty yank. On the stairs above, the tool chest tipped over and started to clunk down the steps.

"What the . . . ?" Harry stared at the loop of rope in his hands and the hole in the door.

"Hey, listen." Marv pressed his ear to the door.

Harry also pressed his ear to the door.

Clank-a-clank-a-clank! The tool chest was picking up speed as it rolled down the stairs.

"What's that sound?" Harry asked.

WHAM! The tool chest smashed into the door, knocking it off its hinges.

CRUNCH! The door flew backwards, crushing the bad guys into the wall.

Clack! The door fell away, leaving Harry and Marv embedded in the wall.

"I think," Marv moaned, "that was the sound of a tool chest falling down the stairs."

While the bad guys pried themselves out of the wall, Kevin ran up the stairs to the roof where he'd left a long coil of thick rope soaking in a bucket of kerosene. One end of the rope was tied around a hundred-pound bag of cement. Kevin pulled on a pair of work gloves and threw the rest of the rope over the side of the building. Then he climbed over the edge of the roof and carefully lowered himself down the rope to the scaffolding beside the first floor.

Harry and Marv staggered up the stairs.

"I don't care if I get the chair," Harry swore as he lugged the green gym bag filled with cash. "I'm gonna kill that kid."

"If we can catch him," Marv said.

"We'll catch him," Harry said. "He's on the roof. Where's he gonna go?"

"Last time he went to a tree house," Marv said.

Harry reached the top of the stairs and kicked open the roof door.

"Surrender, kid!" he shouted, stepping out into the cold, dark night air.

Marv looked around the roof. "I don't see him, Harry."

"I'm down here, you morons!" Kevin shouted from the scaffolding below.

Harry and Marv ran to the edge of the roof and looked down.

Kevin waved and yelled. "Nice night for a neck injury!"

"Let's get him," Marv shouted, grabbing the thick rope. But before he climbed over the roof edge, Harry slapped him on the head.

"Are you nuts?" Harry asked. "That's exactly what he wants us to do. You got a memory?"

"What're you talking about?" Marv asked.

"Look." Marv pointed at the end of the rope tied to the bag of cement. "He's smart, but not smart enough. A hundred pounds of cement. It'll hold the kid. It ain't gonna hold us. We get on the rope and we'll go straight down."

"So what do we do?" Marv asked.

"We'll just have to disappoint the little creep." Harry untied the rope from the bag and knotted it securely around a vent pipe. Then he grabbed the rope and started to lower himself over the side of the building.

"Harry, you're a genius," Marv said admiringly as he followed his partner over the side.

On the scaffolding below, Kevin watched the two bad guys lower themselves down the rope alongside the brownstone. This is going to be good, he thought as he struck a kitchen match against a brick.

Two stories above, as Marv inched down the rope, he started to smell something strange. "Hey, Harry, you wearing after-shave?"

"What're you talking about?" Harry asked below him.

"I smell something," said Marv.

"That ain't after-shave." Harry stopped and took a whiff. "It's kerosene. The rope's soaked in it."

"Why would somebody soak a rope in kerosene?" Marv asked.

Below them, Kevin had the answer. He held the brightly glowing match to the bottom of the rope. "Merry Christmas, guys!"

Harry watched in horror as the bottom of the kerosene-soaked rope burst into flames. "Go up!" he screamed.

Instantly, Marv and Harry started wriggling upward like two giant caterpillars, but the soaked rope was slippery and the flames raced up faster than the bad guys could. On the scaffolding, Kevin quickly checked to make sure the planks of wood and open cans of varnish were in position for the final bombing.

Then he grabbed his backpack, jumped down to the sidewalk, and ran toward the park.

The flames continued to streak up the rope. A second later Kevin heard screams as Marv and Harry let go and crashed down through the loose wooden planks of the scaffolding, catapulting the pails of varnish high into the air. As the bad guys landed in the small garden below the scaffolding, they stared up in horror at the thick brown plume of varnish arching above them.

Splash! The varnish poured down, soaking them to the skin.

CLUNK! CLUNK! They were each smashed on the head with an empty varnish can.

Christmas Eve
Near Central Park
10:35 P.M.

At the corner opposite the park, Kevin ran up to a pay phone and quickly punched 911. He was out of breath and his heart was pounding. The most dangerous part of OPERATION HO! HO! HO! was about to begin. Across the street in the park, the dark tree branches were filled with pigeons, but Kevin was too preoccupied to notice.

"Nine-one-one," an operator answered.

"Quick!" Kevin gasped. "The two guys that robbed Duncan's Toy Chest are in Central Park at Ninety-sixth Street! Hurry! They've got a gun!"

Kevin hung up and looked back down the block. Marv and Harry had just crawled out of the garden in front of Uncle Rob's house. Their clothes were tattered and dripping with varnish

136

and their heads were battered with bumps and bruises.

"Hey! I'm down here," Kevin yelled and waved. "Come and get me before I call the cops!"

As the bad guys started running toward him, Kevin crossed the street in front of the park entrance. He reached the curb and jumped up onto the sidewalk, not noticing a slick dark patch of ice. *Whoops!* He slipped and fell. The strap of his backpack tore and the bag flew a dozen feet away.

Kevin tried to get to his feet, but the ice was slippery and he lost his balance again. He had to get the bag. Inside were the photos of the bad guys in Duncan's Toy Chest and the tape Kevin had made with the Talkboy of Marv discussing the plans for the robbery.

As Kevin scrambled over the ice, he could hear the bad guys' footsteps coming closer. Finally he reached the bag and grabbed it. He was just turning to run into the park when he felt a hand close around his collar and yank him back.

The next thing Kevin knew, he was staring at Harry's bruised and swollen face. The smell of varnish and burned kerosene filled his nostrils. An evil grin spread across the bad guy's cracked and blistered lips.

"Let's go for a stroll, kid." Harry started to drag Kevin into the park. Marv followed behind, keeping an eye out for trouble.

A few moments later, near the very same rocks where Kevin had hid earlier that night, Harry slammed him to the ground and ripped the backpack out of his hands. He opened the bag and dug out the Polaroids Kevin had taken of them robbing Duncan's Toy Chest.

"This'll look nice in the family album," Harry said, slipping the photos into the green gym bag filled with cash. He took out the Talkboy and pressed the "play" button. Marv's voice came out:

"Tonight we're hittin' Duncan's Toy Chest. Five floors of cash."

Harry glared at his partner. "Didn't I tell you to keep your mouth shut?"

"Hey?" Marv said. "How did I know he was recording me?"

"Well, it don't matter now," Harry said, taking out the cassette and putting it in his pocket.

"Yeah," Marv said, looking at Kevin, who was still on the ground. "You may have won the battle, little dude. But you lost the war."

Harry grabbed Kevin by the neck and yanked him up. "You oughtn't not mess around with us, pal. We can be dangerous."

Kevin practically choked as Harry kept a tight grip on his throat and lifted him off the ground.

"Want to burn his hair off?" Harry asked Marv.

"How about we rip it off?" Marv replied.

"Or throw him in a basement?" Harry suggested.

"No," said Marv. "Let's bomb him with a sewer pipe."

Harry's grip was tightening around Kevin's neck. Kicking his feet helplessly in the air, Kevin tried vainly to pry the bad guy's fingers off. Suddenly he saw something that made him stop struggling. Harry had taken out his gun.

"I got a better idea," Harry said with a nasty grin.

The barrel of the gun glinted in the moonlight as Harry raised it toward Kevin. Kevin's heart was pounding a mile a minute and he could hardly breathe. He was so scared he didn't notice that the trees around him were starting to fill up with pigeons.

But Marv did. "Uh, Harry?"

"Shut up," Harry snapped. Kevin stared straight down the barrel of the gun.

"Maybe we better get outa here," Marv said nervously as he stared up at the trees. "Something's strange."

"I said shut up," Harry snapped. He looked down the gun's sight at Kevin. "I never got past the sixth grade, kid. Looks like you won't either."

Harry cocked the gun. Kevin closed his eyes and held his breath.

Suddenly someone said, "Let him go." Kevin felt Harry's grip on his neck loosen. He opened his eyes. The pigeon lady was standing behind the bad guys with a bucket in her hands. Before Harry or Marv could react, she swung the bucket, showering them with birdseed. Most of it stuck to the varnish, making the bad guys look like two giant bird treats.

The sound of hundreds of flapping wings filled the air as the huge flock of hungry pigeons attacked. Harry and Marv screamed and dove to the ground. In an instant they were covered by an army of pecking pigeons. Now the wailing of sirens joined the screams and flapping wings as police cars with lights flashing poured into the park and screeched to a halt.

A dozen policemen jumped out and surrounded the two bad guys, who were almost invisible beneath the swirling mound of pigeons feeding on them. One of the cops raised his gun and fired.

POW! In an instant the startled pigeons were aloft, leaving the two terrified bad guys trembling on the ground. Kevin and the others stared in amazement as Harry and Marv staggered to their feet and put their hands over their heads. They were covered from head to foot with pigeon feathers.

"Look at this." A cop had found the green gym bag. Inside was the stolen money, the photos

Kevin had taken, and the cassette of Marv planning the crime. Kevin watched as Marv and Harry were handcuffed and read their rights.

"You guys should have started a little earlier today," one of the cops said as he pushed them toward the squad car. "The prisoners have already exchanged gifts."

"We would've started earlier," Marv started to explain. "But we had to hide out until the store closed."

"Why don't you just shut up?" Harry shouted, and kicked Marv in the leg. "Didn't the cop just say we got the right to remain silent?"

The cop shoved Harry into the back of the squad car. As Marv bent down to follow him into the car, he turned to the cop.

"My partner's still a little cranky," Marv explained. "We just broke out of jail a few days ago."

The cop pushed Marv in beside Harry. Suddenly there was a loud thumping sound and Marv yelped in pain. Then the door slammed.

From his perch on a nearby rock, Kevin smiled. OPERATION HO! HO! HO! was a complete success. He was just about to thank the police when he remembered that he was still wanted for credit card fraud. Maybe it was better if he just slipped away into the dark.

CHRISTMAS EVE
THE PLAZA HOTEL
11:15 P.M.

In the extra large suite at the Plaza, Kate sat
by the window, staring out into the dark New
York night, wondering where her little boy was
and if he was all right. Her other children were
sprawled asleep on the bed and floor around her.
Peter was slumped in a chair, snoring lightly.
Unable to sleep, Kate sighed and looked down
at the complimentary hotel magazine on her lap.
It was almost midnight and she felt helpless and
very, very sad.

Not far away, Kevin wandered along the dark
cold empty streets feeling the same way. For a
while he'd felt really good about helping to cap-
ture the bad guys and returning the money

meant for the Children's Hospital. But as the hour grew late he once again felt like a lost kid in New York with no place to go and no one to be with. He was glad he'd done his good deed, but it seemed as if it still wasn't enough to erase all the bad ones that had preceded it.

Outside St. Patrick's Cathedral, he stopped and looked up at the tall spires as the bells rang in Christmas. From inside he could hear the choir singing "Joy to the World." But there was no joy in Kevin's world tonight. He bent his head down and kept walking.

In the hotel room, Kate turned another page of the magazine and stared down at a full-page photo of the Rockefeller Center Christmas tree, adorned with lights, tinsel, and decorations. She'd always wanted Kevin to see it.

Then, suddenly, she had the oddest feeling . . .

Kevin also had an odd feeling . . . as if he were being drawn somewhere. He crossed Fifth Avenue, went around a corner, and found himself staring up at the biggest, most beautiful Christmas tree he'd ever seen. Kevin looked at it in awe. Somehow he sensed that it was no accident that he'd found his way to this place. And yet, when he looked around, he saw that he was still alone.

"Maybe I don't deserve a Christmas even if I did do a good deed," he said, gazing sadly at the huge five-pointed gold star at the top of the tree. "But if I can get anything, I don't want any presents. All I want is to take back every mean thing I ever said to my family. Even if they don't take back the things they said to me. I don't care. I love all of them. Even Buzz."

Kevin took a deep breath and watched the vapor leave his lips. As the church bells rang in the distance, he knew there was more he wanted to say: "Listen, if it isn't possible to see all of them, could I just see my mother? I swear I'll never want another thing as long as I live. I just want my mother. I know I won't see her tonight, but just promise me I can see her again sometime . . . anytime. Even if it's just once for only a couple of minutes. Because I need to tell her I'm sorry."

Kevin waited for a moment, as if hoping that by some miracle his wish would come true. But even he was old enough to know it wouldn't. Then he lowered his head. The cold wind picked up some loose newspapers and swirled them around him in a circle. He was just about to walk away when he thought he noticed something. The church bells sounded different. Closer, but smaller.

Kevin slowly turned around. Standing fifty feet from him was a woman who looked an awful lot like his mother. And she was ringing a bell. It looked like she was smiling at him. Kevin rubbed his eyes and looked again. It couldn't be, could it?

"Mom?" he gasped in a hoarse whisper.

Kate put the silver bell back in her pocket and stepped toward her son. She felt tears start to roll down her cheeks. "Merry Christmas, sweetheart."

As Kevin ran toward his mother, he thought of the wish he'd just made and looked back at the tree in amazement. Wow! he thought. That worked fast!

A moment later Kate kneeled down and hugged him tightly.

"How'd you know I was here?" Kevin asked.

"I know you and Christmas trees," Kate said as she rubbed a tear out of her eye.

"I guess this is the biggest one around, huh?" Kevin said.

Kate smiled. "Let's go tell Dad you're all right."

"Where's everyone else?" Kevin asked.

"At the hotel," Kate said, sliding her arm around his shoulders.

"They're in New York?" Kevin gasped, wide-eyed.

Kate smiled. "They didn't like the palm trees either."

CHRISTMAS MORNING
DUNCAN'S TOY CHEST
1 A.M.

E. F. Duncan stood on the sidewalk wearing a suit and a gray cashmere topcoat. His wife stood beside him, clutching his arm, dressed in an emerald green gown covered by a brown mink coat. They'd been called away from a Christmas party by the police, and now watched quietly as two glaziers replaced the broken window of the store.

Inside, a team of evidence specialists combed through the broken glass and mangled cash registers looking for clues to the crime. The Duncans knew that a great deal of cash had been stolen, money that was supposed to go to the Children's Hospital.

Suddenly a police car pulled up in front of the store and a cop jumped out.

"It's all over, Mr. Duncan," he said.

Duncan frowned. "What do you mean?"

"We apprehended the thieves and recovered your money."

Mr. Duncan's jaw dropped and his wife squeezed his arm with delight.

"Thank you," he said, happily shaking the officer's hand. "Thank you very much!"

The cop went back to his car. Mr. Duncan and his wife were about to go home when one of the evidence specialists approached him carrying a brick and an envelope. "Excuse me, are you Mr. Duncan?"

"Yes?" Duncan turned, surprised.

The specialist pulled the envelope from the brick and handed it to him. "We found this inside. Looks like a kid broke your window."

Duncan looked down at the envelope and frowned. It was addressed to him in a child's handwriting. He tore it open and found a letter written on a sheet of Plaza Hotel stationery:

Dear Mr. Duncan,

    I broke your window to catch the bad guys. I'm sorry. Do you have insurance? If you don't, I'll send you some money when it snows some more (if I ever get back to Chicago).

             Merry Christmas,
             Kevin McCallister

Mrs. Duncan tugged on her husband's coat sleeve. "What is it, dear?"

E. F. Duncan smiled and said, "Turtle-doves."

CHRISTMAS MORNING
THE PLAZA HOTEL
7 A.M.

The sky was gray at dawn. Up in the McCallister's suite, Kevin slept in a double bed with Fuller and Brooke. The other McCallisters were spread out on the floor and in the living room. Suddenly Fuller opened his eyes and sat up.

"Holy smokes!" he gasped excitedly. "It's Christmas morning!"

Next to him, Kevin rubbed his eyes and yawned. "Don't get your hopes up."

Fuller looked puzzled. "Why not?"

"I'm not sure Santa Claus goes to hotels," Kevin said, a little sadly.

"Are you nuts?" Fuller replied. "He's omnipresent. He goes everywhere."

Fuller jumped out of bed and started yelling, "Wake up, everyone! It's Christmas!"

All around the suite Kevin could hear people grumbling as Fuller woke them up. Maybe a hotel wasn't the greatest place in the world to have Christmas, but at least Kevin was back with his family and that's what mattered most.

Suddenly he heard gasps and startled exclamations coming from the foyer of the suite. Curious, he got out of bed and went to look. At first he couldn't see anything because the whole McCallister clan had crowded into the small foyer. But as he squeezed past them he found himself staring at a beautiful Christmas tree surrounded by more gifts than he'd ever seen.

"Wow!" Kevin gasped.

He couldn't imagine where it all had come from, but then he spotted the decorations celebrating the twelve days of Christmas . . . the same decorations he'd seen on the tree in Duncan's Toy Chest.

"Are we in the right room?" Buzz asked in amazement.

"Get the camera!" Uncle Frank cried.

Fuller and Brooke waded into the sea of gifts and started tearing open the presents.

"Careful with the wrapping paper," Aunt Leslie warned them. "We can reuse it."

The other members of the family started to reach for the gifts, but suddenly Buzz raised his arms and shouted, "Stop, everyone!"

They turned and stared at him.

"Listen," Buzz said. "If Kevin hadn't screwed things up so bad again we wouldn't be in this most perfect and huge hotel room with a truckload of free stuff. So it's only fair that he gets to open the first present. Then I'll go, and then the rest of you."

Buzz bent down and picked up a big box covered with green and red wrapping paper and handed it to Kevin. "Merry Christmas, Kev."

Everyone started to applaud. Kevin took a bow and then started to open the present. But something didn't feel right. Suddenly he realized what it was, and ran back to the bedroom. He found his blue coat and felt the pockets. The turtledoves Mr. Duncan had given him were still there.

A little while later Kevin walked into Central Park, wearing his coat over his pajamas. Ahead he saw the pigeon lady tossing seed to a hundred hungry pigeons on the ground around her.

"Merry Christmas!" Kevin waved at her.

The pigeon lady scowled, then smiled. "Merry Christmas, Kevin."

Kevin stepped through the sea of birds, then took the seed bucket from her and set it down. He opened her dirty hand and put one of the turtledoves in it. The pigeon lady looked con-

151

fused, so Kevin showed her his turtledove.

"Now I have one and you have one," he explained. "As long as we each have a turtledove, we're friends forever."

The pigeon lady blinked with surprise. "Thank you, Kevin."

Kevin gave her a hug. "I won't forget you. Trust me."

"I do," the pigeon lady said with a big smile.

Kevin smiled back. Everything had worked out great. The kids at the Children's Hospital would get their money. His family got all those presents from Mr. Duncan. The pigeon lady now had someone she could trust . . .

And as for Kevin, well, he didn't really need to get anything. Except the satisfaction of knowing that after all was said and done, it really was the thought that counts.

About the Author

Todd Strasser has written many award-winning novels for young and teenaged readers. He is a frequent speaker at junior and senior high schools, and conferences. He and his wife and children live in Westchester County, New York, and try to avoid the city during the holidays.